"The guy in that car back there—"

"Andrew Brogg," Brian finished, that cold stone of worry dropping into his stomach once more. "And he's doing a feature on Guardian Paws?"

"That's what he says."

Brian understood that Angela didn't trust Brogg, and he didn't, either. But he had cause. He'd been warned that the reporter seemed to have been following them as recently as the day he'd met Angela. Conceited as it seemed, Brian was positive the reporter's interest in Guardian Paws was solely related to Brian's connection to them.

Angela didn't deserve any negative fallout as a result of his own problems. But his ability to release the story of his sight loss the way he wanted to was spinning out of control....

Books by Sharon Mignerey

Love Inspired Suspense

Through the Fire
Small Town Secrets
Shadows of Truth
From the Ashes
The Good Neighbor

SHARON MIGNEREY

After living most of her life in Colorado, Sharon recently moved to the Texas Gulf coast where she found that Southern hospitality lived up to its reputation for being warm and welcoming. She's always known that she wanted to be a storyteller from the time she learned that spelling words could be turned into stories. Sharon's first book was published in 1997 after winning RWA's Golden Heart award in 1995. That same book went on to win the National Readers' Choice Award. In addition to writing novels, Sharon has had several articles published by *The Writer* magazine. She says the accolades are wonderful, but the only lasting satisfaction comes from serving the work. When she's not writing, you can find her happily involved with her critique group, learning how to garden in the Texas heat, or playing with her two dogs.

Sharon loves hearing from readers. She can be reached either through her website, www.sharonmignerey.com, or in care of Love Inspired Books, 233 Broadway, Suite 1001, New York, NY 10279.

From the Ashes

Sharon Mignerey

Love Inspired

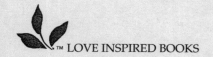

Recycling programs
for this product may
not exist in your area.

™ LOVE INSPIRED BOOKS

ISBN-13: 978-0-373-78755-5

FROM THE ASHES

For we walk by faith, not by sight.
—*2 Corinthians* 5:7

In memory of my mother, Thelma Anis Black

Acknowledgments

My deepest gratitude goes to the Clinton family—
Willie Jr., Sajuana and Shanelle,
who so generously shared their experiences with
sight loss, especially their wonderful stories about
Willie's guide dogs, Jada (his current dog)
and Elton (who is now retired).

I also need to thank Russ Burcham, M.D.,
who patiently answered my questions
concerning glaucoma and sight loss—
if there are mistakes in the book, they are mine
and are no reflection on him. A special thank-you
to my proofreader, Danielle, whose sharp eyes
and attention to detail are invaluable.

ONE

"Hey, doll face."

It was a nickname—and a voice—Angela London had never wanted to hear again. She searched the crowd for the man who had betrayed her. There he was leaning against the wall near a drinking fountain, looking as though he belonged—which he didn't. Looking as though he could be one of the businessmen leaving the monthly luncheon for the chamber of commerce—which he wasn't. Any business he had would be on the shady side of the law.

Tommy Manderoll was dead last on any list of people she wanted to see. Smiling as though he were welcome, he started toward her.

"Angela," a woman said, coming to a stop next to her. "Thanks so much for your talk. The work you're doing is so needed. Wonderful, really." She patted Polly, wearing her service-dog-in-training vest and sitting at Angela's feet, then pressed a check into her hand. "You're making such a difference with Guardian Paws."

"I hope so." She glanced down at the check, the donation beyond generous. "Thank you. You're sure you wouldn't rather put this in the prepaid envelope that was in your packet?"

She shook her head. "I'm giving that to my boss." The woman squeezed her arm and moved away.

"You are the woman of the hour," Tommy said, coming to a stop in front of her, adjusting his tie in a gesture of preening that was second nature to him. "The outfit almost goes with the dog."

There wasn't a single thing wrong with the taupe, tailored, below-the-knee skirt and knit twinset she was wearing, but she still took the statement as an insult. This was the new Angela London, the one who didn't like men like Tommy Manderoll and who didn't wear the flashy clothes that attracted them.

She was prevented from answering when a deep voice inquired, "Miss London?"

The vaguely familiar-looking man who approached her was tall, with broad shoulders and a chiseled face that would have been perfect in a razor commercial. He offered his hand. She automatically took it and had the fleeting thought that his smile was meant only for her as his broad palm enveloped her smaller hand.

"Being here today was an answer to a prayer," he said. "But you probably hear that all the time. I'm Brian Ramsey."

"Nice to meet you." The name, like his face, was familiar, though she couldn't have said from where. Probably thirtysomething, though his eyes seemed older somehow. The niggle that she should know him, or at least know of him, didn't go away as she took in his aura of confidence and the superb fit of his sports coat.

"I need a dog." An indefinable expression chased across his face, and he took a breath before asking, "When would be a good time to call you?"

"That's something I'd like to know, too," Tommy interrupted. "*Miss London,* when would be a good time to call?"

Angela looked from Brian to her ex-boyfriend, the man she had never wanted to see again.

"I'm sorry," Brian said. "I've caught you at a bad time—"

"No." Angela touched the back of his hand when he would have walked away. She swallowed against the giddy feeling that heated her cheeks when his tawny, golden-brown gaze settled on her face. "Do you have a card so I can call you?"

"Sure." Shifting his wool top coat to the other arm, he retrieved a slim wallet from his navy sports coat and pulled out a card. "I look forward to hearing from you." Then, glancing down at Polly, he asked, "What kind of dog is she?"

"Since she was adopted from the pound when she was six months old, it's hard to know for sure. She's certainly got some golden retriever in her and probably some shepherd."

"She looks just about perfect."

"Thanks. I think she is." Angela grinned.

As if reluctant to leave, Brian took one step away, then turned back. "You *will* call, won't you?"

"By tomorrow morning at the latest," she promised.

He nodded once, then strode down the hall, keeping her attention on him even as Tommy said, "Brian

Ramsey is way out of your league. If you think a pro ballplayer, even a retired loser like him, would give you the time of day, you're dead wrong."

Brian Ramsey certainly had the physique of an athlete, but since she didn't follow sports, she had no idea what team he had played for.

"So you're into dogs now." Tommy moved into her line of vision. "I would have never figured that."

"What do you want?" She finally looked at him, not caring how rude or blunt her question was. When Tommy crowded into her space, she moved back a step.

He clucked his tongue. "Now is that any way to talk to an old friend?"

"You're no friend," she said softly, "and I'm not sure you ever were."

"Don't tell me you're holding a grudge." He drew her toward the edge of the rotunda as a group of people came out of the banquet room. Next to her, Polly stayed right at her side, standing patiently as she had been trained to do.

Angela met his gaze square on, once more putting some space between them and lowering her voice to a murmur. "How would you define turning state's evidence so you got to walk away scot free while I was sentenced to four years in prison?" Thankfully, she'd had to serve only two, and they had been the longest of her life. The only good thing out of that experience was that she had been chosen to be part of a pilot program to train service dogs who had needed a second chance as much as the female inmates.

"I did what I had to do," Tommy said, his smile fading.

"So, I repeat, what do you want?"

He glanced around the hallway where people had gathered in groups of two or three and many others were still making their way toward the wide doorway that led to the parking lot. "Let's go get a drink somewhere."

Angela shook her head.

"Ah. You've got the dog."

Her gaze fell to Polly. "That. Plus, I don't drink."

He smiled and shook his head. "Pull the other leg, doll face. We both know you do."

"Don't call me that." She held up a hand. "I'm not going anywhere with you."

He took a step closer to her, bent his head toward hers, and pulled the check the woman had given her a few minutes earlier from her hand. "I don't know why you're messing around with pocket change like this when you've got a half million dollars stashed away."

That again. The same rumored money that she had supposedly stolen from a drug kingpin.

At last she understood why he had looked her up. The promise of easy money. If Tommy was good at anything, it was looking after his own best interests to the exclusion of anyone else.

She took back the check and stepped away from him. "There is no money, Tommy. Never was." The rumor of it, though, had nearly cost her best friend her life. That was one more regret Angela had to live with.

"I don't believe you." He shrugged. "I've got a sure

thing, and you're just the kind of girl who would want in."

The statement was a replay of a conversation they'd had a long time ago. Then, a whole lifetime ago, she had been exactly that kind of girl. *Girl*. She was no longer young or naive in any way at all.

"Sorry, no."

He ducked his head toward her a little, pasting on the cajoling smile that once had worked on her. "It'll be like old times—"

Once more, she lowered her voice, but she couldn't keep the anger from it as she said, "You mean like the old times where you showed me how to party and then supplied the drugs that I sold for you so I could pay for my own habit? You mean like the old times when I'd do anything for you, no matter how stupid?"

"Settle down." He looked around, then, evidently satisfied he couldn't be heard, he said, "Look at you. You're the girl who likes sexy silk and trips to Cabo and European wheels. This isn't the real you."

"Actually, it is."

"I don't believe that, either."

"I don't much care what you believe as long as you do it someplace else. And as for getting involved in any of your 'sure' things—you've got to be kidding."

"Then at least stake me the money. You know I'll pay you back."

"Stab me in the back is more like it," she said, his sense of entitlement typical and irritating. "Same answer as before. No. As in no way, never. C'mon, Polly." She took a single step, then turned back toward him.

"Goodbye, Tommy. And I mean that in the most final way possible."

"You're gonna regret not taking me up on the offer," he said, his cocky grin returning, his voice loud enough to carry as though she had just turned him down on a business deal.

In fact, she had.

"And you'll regret ever bothering me again," she said, tugging on Polly's leash and moving away from him. She realized her voice had carried to a couple of the people around them when they turned and looked at her.

He took a threatening step toward her, his hand curling around her elbow to keep her from moving away, his pleasant smile masking his fierce whisper. "That sounded too much like a threat." His grip tightened. "Remember this, doll face. You went to prison because you had no guts. Don't be making threats you can't keep."

She pulled her arm away, proud of herself that she wasn't cowering the way she once had. "That was no threat. It was a promise. Stay away from me."

"A promise for you." He pressed two fingers against his lips, kissed them, and tossed it toward her. "I'll be seeing you."

He walked away from her, as though he didn't have a care in the world, as though he hadn't just shaken hers. What she had ever seen in him? A stupid question since she had promised herself more honesty than that. He'd been an easy end to getting the drugs that had consumed her. *Had* being the operative word.

Her getaway wasn't as clean as she would have liked. Several people who had attended the luncheon and watched her demonstration with Polly approached her the instant Tommy left. They asked thoughtful questions and a few people, like the first woman, gave her a donation. Through it, she kept noticing Tommy lurking in the background, which kept her thinking about his demand for money.

The kingpin who had been Tommy's supplier had coerced her into using the business she'd owned with her best friend, Rachel, as a means to launder money. For reasons Angela still didn't understand, after she'd gone to prison he'd decided she had stolen a half million from him that she'd left with Rachel. Angela's pastor had encouraged her to forgive herself. She didn't know how she could. Her own greed had ruined a friendship that still meant everything to her. The price Rachel had paid was unbearable to Angela.

Until today, she had believed that Tommy was behind the rumor. Except he wouldn't be trying to shake her down for the money if he had been. Right now, Angela knew only two things for sure. She wanted that part of her life behind her and she never wanted to see Tommy again.

She shouldn't have been surprised that he'd shown up today, she decided. Usually, the events of her day were a reflection of her daily Bible study. This morning's reading had been from the first book of Proverbs, a warning of what happens to those who throw in with bad company. *My child, if sinners try to seduce you, do not go with them.* Only, a lifetime ago she had, and, caught in the lure of money and drugs, she had deliberately harmed her best friend. That simple, awful act had come back to her tenfold. Now, she doubted she would ever be able to make things right again. God might have forgiven her sins, but she was a long way from forgiving herself.

She might have paid her debt to society as defined by her prison term and her just-ended year of parole, but she still had debts to repay and would for the rest of her life, the least of them monetary. As always, that thought was nearly overwhelming, which made the idea of her having the money Tommy wanted all the more ludicrous.

One day at a time, she whispered to herself. One minute at a time.

She went outside and immediately wished she had remembered to put on a coat when she had dashed out of the house hours ago. The summerlike temperatures this morning had disappeared into the more typical November day in Denver—blustery with the scent of snow in the air, the cold biting right through her. The walk to the bus stop was going to be cold, as was the walk the rest of the way home on the other end.

A couple of hotel workers, bundled against the cold, were wrapping Christmas lights around the trunks of the trees flanking the entrance.

To her surprise, Brian Ramsey was coming toward the door, smiling—that same warm-down-to-her-toes smile that he had given her before.

"I was hoping I'd catch you before you took off,"

Brian said. "I know you said you'd call, but if we could talk today, that would be better."

Angela shivered as a gust of wind hit them, and Brian immediately noticed she wasn't wearing a coat.

Her expression had gone from distracted to interested when her gaze lit on him. That at least was something.

"Is your car far?" He shrugged out of his cashmere top coat and settled it over her shoulders. The coat was huge on her, but somehow looked right, too. When she shivered once more, he reached out and closed the top button to keep the coat from slipping off her slim shoulders.

"Actually, we rode the bus today. I was headed for the Park and Ride across the street." She glanced at him. "I should have known better than to leave home without a coat."

"The weather can turn on a dime," he agreed, looking from her to her destination, turning his head to compensate for his lack of peripheral vision. "Across the street" didn't come close to describing the long walk across the hotel parking lot, up a hill and across another parking lot to the bus stop. There, she still wouldn't have any protection from the weather except for a glass-enclosed lean-to.

"Look, you don't know me from Adam," he said, "but I'd be happy to give you a lift wherever you'd like to go." This close, he became aware of her fragrance—soft, mysterious. Her soft brown hair had slipped from the clip holding it up, and tendrils curled around her face. When he'd watched her demonstration, he'd thought she was in her early twenties. Now he pegged her age at least ten years older, though nothing about those years made her any less appealing.

"And you'd be able to tell me what's on your mind," she allowed, "since you said you needed a dog."

"That's right." He waited while she searched his face without any apparent recognition. Given all the notoriety he'd recently had, finding one person who didn't know him on sight was a relief. "I'm harmless, I promise."

She grinned. "So said the spider to the fly."

He liked her sense of humor. "Probably. But if you're not going to go with me, I want my coat back. It's cold."

Once more her eyes danced, and she patted the dog on the head. "What do you think, Polly? A warm ride or a cold walk?"

The dog wagged its tail, and Angela looked back at him. He heard the quick beep of a horn, and he turned his head, taking in the vehicle he had stopped driving two months ago easing up to the curb. "My car is here," Brian said, pointing at his Escalade. His driver waved.

"Okay," she said, stepping off the curb. "I am supposed to know you from somewhere, though, aren't I?"

He waited until they had reached the vehicle and opened the back door for her before saying, "That depends, I guess, on whether you read the sports pages."

She gave him another of those considering glances with her expressive brown eyes. "Not usually."

He opened the back door, and as the dog jumped in, motioned to Sam. "Say hi to Sam Waite."

"Hey," Sam said.

"Hi," Angela responded, taking the arm Brian offered for support as she climbed into the backseat.

He went around the vehicle to sit in the backseat with her, and, realizing his intention, she signaled the dog to climb into the back of the vehicle.

"Where are we off to?" Sam asked after they were settled.

"The lady's pleasure," Brian said.

"In that case San Diego. At least it would be warmer there." She smiled at Sam's raised eyebrows and cheerful expression, then gave him her address, adding the directions.

The address was far enough out in Denver's northeast suburbs that Brian doubted it was on any direct bus routes. He wondered if the choice was part of the dog's training.

After they were underway, he figured she'd ask why he had a driver, but she didn't. Instead, she said, "That sounded rude. You know, saying I don't usually read about sports."

"Not rude." He didn't like that he had put his career behind him on something less than his own terms, but he also knew that simply because sports had consumed him from the day he could walk, it wasn't so for many others. "Truthful."

"You're a ball player?"

He nodded, allowing a grin. Ball player left a lot of room.

"Football?" she ventured.

"What makes you say so?" he asked.

"You're tall, but you don't have that seven-foot height

that seems to go these days with basketball players." Her gaze left him and strayed to the gray day outside.

"You left off baseball or soccer."

She shook her head with a good-natured grin. "I'm sticking to my first guess."

"You're right. I played football."

"What team? Or maybe I'm supposed to ask what position."

"I'm a quarterback. *Was* a quarterback," he said.

"Are you completely insulted that I don't know?"

He shook his head. "Since I didn't play here in Denver—"

"Where, then?"

"Boston." He found her watching him as though what he said really did matter. Once he'd been conceited enough to think that it did. "Thankfully, my lousy season last year didn't rate front-page news here."

"This is home?"

"Yep. Born and raised. Graduated from George Washington High School. What about you?"

"Transplant," she said. "I grew up on the Western Slope. Glenwood Springs mostly." She turned slightly in the seat, his large coat still draped over her shoulders. "Why do you need a dog, Brian Ramsey?"

There it was, the bald question that had only a bald answer to go with it. The words didn't come as easily as he wanted though he had been laying the groundwork for months now. This was one more step in the journey, and he liked the exchange he'd been having with her. The three words that answered her question would change everything.

"Are you married?" he asked instead of answering her question. Extending these moments before the inevitable. "Involved with anyone?"

"No." She gave him a challenging look that could have meant he should mind his own business or that she didn't want to be involved.

"Me, neither."

"Good to know," she said, her smile taking the sting out of the words. "What does that have to do with your wanting a dog? We train dogs only for the deaf and the blind as I told you during my speech. Do you want to help a family member?"

He shook his head, studying her, in the middle of another of his daily realizations that everything in this life that he'd taken for granted for so long was precious. Driving. Looking at a pretty girl.

"A friend?" Her eyes really were beautiful. She was close enough that he could see her whole face, even though his field of vision was markedly smaller than it had been a few weeks ago.

"No."

She frowned, drawing his attention to a freckle at the edge of her lip. "Are you all right?"

He took a breath and nodded. "Fine, today." Absorbing all he could of her lovely face, he said, "I'm going blind. The dog is for me."

TWO

Stunned by the news and hoping her expression didn't reveal that, Angela watched Brian look away from her, then back, his own gaze challenging.

"Now you know why I need a driver." He gestured toward Sam.

"Yes." As with every other person she had met who had lost their vision, she knew there was a heartbreaking story here. As a professional athlete in the public eye, Brian would have an extra set of challenges. Not necessarily worse than what others faced. Just different.

His expression was so implacable that she suspected he was waiting for that moment he'd undoubtedly had with others. The outpouring of heartfelt sympathy and the "I'm so sorry." She was, but telling him so would only make him feel pitied. He didn't need that, surely didn't want that.

"The first step is filling out an application, then getting you scheduled for a class—"

"You mean after my sight is totally gone?" He shook his head. "Listen, I know others are ahead of me in that whole process to get a dog. I've done my homework, and I know about the two-year training stint. And I know about the preparation and class work that I need to do ahead of time. The thing is, I'm in a unique situation here—"

"Privileged?" She hadn't intended to interrupt, but the idea that he might think he could circumvent the system simply because he had money made her suddenly, unreasonably annoyed. With that, she became aware of the vehicle's leather interior and the latest in gadgets on the dashboard. With his wealth, why was he seeking her help?

"Fortunately, yes," he said simply. "But that's not what I mean. To me, having this warning that I'm losing my vision is like training camp. You've got a set of things you need to do to get ready for the season—get in shape, learn the new playbook, do the work to build a team out of a bunch of individuals. What I'm going through is the same thing." His expression lightened. "A Braille playbook isn't going to be easy to learn."

Surprised at his ready agreement to being privileged and intrigued by his comparison to training season, Angela saw the passion in him that had undoubtedly driven him to become an athlete good enough to be a professional.

"Exactly what do you want from Guardian Paws?" she asked, her annoyance diffused by his explanation.

"To participate in picking out and training my guide dog."

Like his statement about going blind, this one was equally forthright, as though he had given the idea a lot of thought.

"Why Guardian Paws?" she asked. "There are other organizations, more experienced trainers—"

"Who could help me?"

His gaze searched her face, making her wonder just how much of his sight was left and what was causing his loss of vision. Diabetes? Macular degeneration? Glaucoma? Some irreversible injury?

"First, you're local, so it seems reasonable that the logistics would be easier. Second, because your organization is small, I'm hoping you'll be able—willing—to take a chance on this."

"So you've already asked one of the other schools."

"Several." He nodded. "They have a set protocol that works, and I understand that."

Sam turned the SUV onto her street.

"You've given me a lot to think about," she said to Brian. "I've got to talk with my partner."

"Is this the right house?" Sam asked from the driver's seat.

Angela looked out at the small ranch-style home where she lived. Her twelve-year-old Honda Civic was in the driveway. "Yes."

He pulled into the driveway, then got out of the car to open the door for her. She unbuttoned Brian's overcoat and left it on the seat as she got out of the car. A gust of wind hit her, and she shivered.

On the other side Brian was getting out, as well. Like the well-trained dog she was, Polly waited for her command before hopping out of the back of the SUV and immediately coming to stand next to Angela.

"Thanks for the ride," she said as Brian walked her to the door.

"I should be thanking you for listening," he said. "Anything you need from me to help you make a decision—" He laughed suddenly. "Well, make a decision that I like."

"I'll call you." She smiled at him, liking the way he turned his humor and his expectations back on himself.

"I'm looking forward to it," he said, heading back down the walk, this time getting into the passenger seat of the SUV.

Another car came slowly down the street, the driver looking in their direction. Angela watched, hoping it wasn't Tommy Manderoll.

It wasn't, and she breathed a sigh of relief as the car drove past her house. Sam backed into the street while Brian gave her a brief salute from the passenger seat as they drove away.

After she let herself into the house, she remembered there had been a newspaper article about him recently. Something non-sports related. Looking through the stack of newspapers she had set aside for recycling, she found the article on the front page of the Family Living section of last Saturday's paper—a huge piece about his foundation and the work he did with inner-city teens. With the loss of public money to fund after-school programs, the foundation had quietly and effectively filled in the gap. Sports was the cornerstone, but there were also activities for kids interested in other things, all designed to build teamwork and burn energy.

"The programs of the Beanstalk Gang are built

around traditional activities, like sports. But we do more than that. Imagine field trips that take these kids behind the scenes where they can see people doing jobs they might aspire to. These outings are styled after reality shows and are fun and require skill," the article quoted Brian. "It's all about being somewhere safe and being where kids know somebody cares about them. You can't let them know that in a sentimental way, of course, so it's all in the guise of competition and learning life skills—teamwork, decision making, sportsmanship. It's about basic tutoring when it's required—you'd be surprised how many of these kids can't read. Compared to the cost of doing nothing, these programs take an insanely small amount of money."

The article concluded saying that he was proof that one person could make a difference.

Indeed. The man was attractive inside and out, a man she could seriously like. And *like* is the furthest it could go, she firmly told herself, imagining the field day a reporter would have if either of them acted on the attraction. Assuming, that is, that her awareness of him hadn't been one-sided.

The convict and the blind quarterback. That was a headline she never wanted to see.

She had been the object of a reporter's insatiable curiosity once before and the means to a front-page story. No way did she want that again.

Despite the warning she had given him that she needed to talk to her partner, Angela expected Maisey Erdmann to go along with the idea of involving Brian in the training of his own dog.

He couldn't know how tempting his offer was. They had narrowed the focus of their training to working with dogs for the blind and the deaf. And they knew they could have the most impact by remaining a small local organization. Angela dreamed of one day having access to dogs specifically bred to be guide dogs, but she'd also had good luck so far with the carefully chosen dogs they had found from the pound and through various rescue organizations. And because they worked with local clients, they could get them involved in the training for six to eight weeks instead of the typical four.

Brian had said he wanted to pick out his own dog, and she had one that she hoped he'd want. She suspected he would hate Jasper on sight, but they would be perfect for each other—two athletes in the midst of a transition.

Just after sunrise the following morning, Angela arrived with Polly at the farm where Guardian Paws did business. Their training facility occupied one small corner of land and included a tiny farmhouse used for the office and a six-stall barn they had converted to a kennel. The barn was new, but its old-fashioned gambrel roof and deliberately faded red paint made it look as though it had been on the property for years.

Tim Warren had donated this part of his farm for them to use, a generous gift that he said was his way of giving back to the community. He farmed the rest of the sixty-acre property, growing organic fruits and vegetables along the Platte River.

In the distance, old-fashioned cornstalk teepees covered the field, Tim's homage to a simpler time. The black soil gleamed with a layer of frost. The place was quiet, unlike summer when everything was growing and people came in all day long to pick their own vegetables. Personally, Angela thought Tim and his wife had been brilliant in their concept. Give their customers the rewards of having a garden without any of the headache of weeding and watering.

The harvest-theme decorations that had lined the driveway had been replaced by garlands of evergreen, along with a sign that counted down the days until the day after Thanksgiving, when Christmas trees would be available for sale.

Angela turned on lights in the house and put on a pot of coffee to brew before heading out the back door to the kennel with Polly obediently close behind. The small barn had a center aisle and three stalls on each side that had been perfect to convert for their purposes. Four of the stalls could hold the dogs, supplies were stored in one and the final one was their examination room.

She turned on the light and was greeted by wagging tails from the four dogs occupying two of the kennels.

"You guys are already awake?" She opened the gates and was immediately surrounded. If any of them had been jealous that Polly had gotten to go home with her last night, none showed it. Instead, they sniffed her in greeting, and when Angela opened the door to their fenced yard, they raced outside.

As happened every single morning, Angela's heart swelled with gratitude. She didn't simply like her job— she loved it.

After hearing about the program to train service dogs shortly after she was sent to prison, she had applied, hoping she'd be chosen. At first, she had imagined it would be a way to fill the time that had loomed endlessly in front of her. Instead, she had found a calling, the work she was meant to do.

Being with the dogs made her thankful, and she felt blessed to have this work. Dogs didn't have an agenda. They didn't have expectations she could never meet. They lived in the moment. Important life lessons, every one.

Prior to the end of her sentence, she had scoured the entire state, looking for someone who would hire her to pursue the calling she had discovered in prison. Not only had Maisey taken her on, she had stunned Angela after her parole was over by making her a partner in the business. It was a gift that Angela cherished, most especially because she knew she hadn't deserved it.

One by one, almost as though taking turns, the dogs ran to her before taking off again. Bailey, the gorgeous golden retriever whose training was just beginning and who had been too high energy for the family who gave her up. Checkers, the smart shepherd–border collie mix who had been found in the pound without any tags. Gatsby, the black Lab mix, who was also a rescue from the pound where he had been taken after being found tied to a tree at a campground in the mountains above Golden. Polly, who was scheduled to begin training with her hearing-impaired master within the next month.

And the dog she had in mind for Brian—Jasper, the year-old elegant standard poodle who had been a socialite's accessory. Maisey had thought Angela was crazy when she asserted that he'd be a wonderful guide dog, since the conventional wisdom was they had to be German shepherds, golden retrievers or Labrador retrievers, but she had signed on to the project with enthusiasm after reading the success stories about other poodles that Angela had uncovered.

"How are you doing, boy?" Angela said to him. He dutifully sat in front of her, his dark eyes on her as she rubbed the tips of his ears, which practically made him smile. Within the first month, he had learned more commands than any other dog she'd ever seen. That had been three months ago, and he continued to be the most responsive dog she had ever worked with. High energy and smart, he was going to need someone who was active and disciplined. To Angela, that sounded exactly like Brian Ramsey.

She had spoken with him briefly last night and suggested that he come out to the farm to meet their dogs in training. He had promised to come late this morning, his voice filled with anticipation and relief as though he somehow knew she was on the verge of agreeing to his proposal. She wondered if he'd be quite so pleased after he met Jasper.

The back door to the house slammed, and Angela turned to see Maisey coming toward her. Fiftyish and plump, the woman was smiling, just as always.

"Every single morning I think I can get here before you, and you've beat me again." She held her bracelet-encased arms out to the dogs who came to greet her.

"I couldn't sleep," Angela said while Maisey murmured greetings to each of the dogs. "So I decided I might as well get up and come in."

"Thinking about that good-looking Brian Ramsey, I bet."

Angela had called her last night before talking to Brian. "Yes, but not because he's good-looking. I invited him out here today so you can meet him. I want to know what you think before we agree to let him participate in the training."

Maisey laughed at her prim tone. "I told you already. I trust your judgment."

"I know you do." Angela headed back toward the kennel to set out breakfast for the dogs. "But let's face it. Since he's a high-profile kind of man, we have to take the bad with the good. If this doesn't work out the way he hopes it will—"

"It's all going to be fine."

"Says the eternal optimist." Angela followed Maisey inside, holding the door open for the dogs.

Maisey headed to the cupboard and set out five dishes. "What are you afraid of?"

Angela stared into space a moment before saying, "I want to make sure it's not my ego with grandiose ideas that makes me think this can work." She began measuring out the kibble for each dish.

"I'll meet him," Maisey promised. "But the choice is still yours." She grabbed a couple of the bowls, setting them in front of Checkers and Gatsby, who like all the dogs were patiently sitting, as they had been trained. "I picked up the messages. There were three for you from a Tommy Manderoll. 'Urgent,' he said."

Angela sighed. "He's a lowlife from my past," she said, setting down the remaining bowls. Just because he had called her didn't mean she had to call him back. She was sure he'd take any contact, even in the form of go-fly-a-kite as some sort of perverse encouragement. "Throw away the messages."

"Anything else I can do?" Maisey asked.

Angela shook her head. "Anything else would be illegal."

Maisey laughed. "Well, we can't have that, can we?"

After the dogs ate, Angela put on their in-training vests, a signal that playtime was over. As she worked with each of the dogs, she made notations in the planning books she kept for each one. She kept thinking about Brian's comparison to training camp.

She supposed the initial assessment they made of the dogs was like training camp—figuring out which ones had the aptitude for their intended jobs. Only a few of the dogs they had chosen for the program had made the grade. The dogs that didn't were adopted out to families. For the dogs that did, the real work began, complete with a "playbook" where goals were set out, progress was charted and personality traits were noted.

When Brian and Sam arrived shortly before noon, Maisey hung around only long enough for introductions before leaving with a whispered, "He's great. Snap him up," behind Brian's back. To Angela, that sounded way too personal. Personal would never do.

Brian told Sam he could leave for a couple of hours, which left Angela alone with him. Gathering several

Frisbees and softballs, she took him to the yard where the dogs were.

"This is playtime?" he asked with a teasing smile. "And here I thought you'd give me a formal demonstration."

"You saw that yesterday at the luncheon," she said, handing him one of the discs. "These guys all love Frisbee and can go at it all day long."

"Good thing I have a strong arm," he said, taking the first one from her and sending it flying. "And that I don't have to worry about interceptions."

"Did that happen a lot?" she asked.

"Too much last year." He threw the next three discs in rapid succession, a big grin on his face as the dogs chased down the yard, their eyes on their prize. "These guys could be NFL-bound with speed like that."

"How did you first learn you were losing your vision?"

The first of the dogs returned and dropped the disc at Brian's feet. "Good boy," he said, patting the dog and throwing the Frisbee again. "I was having the worst headaches of my life. At first the doctor thought it was migraines."

"Glaucoma?"

Brian stared at her, aware that the dogs were returning one by one and dropping their prizes at his feet. "How could you know that?"

"One of the symptoms." She smiled slightly. "And not a huge leap since it's a primary cause of blindness. It's pretty unusual for someone your age, but not unheard of."

He picked up the Frisbees and threw them one by one for the dogs already running away from him like well-honed running backs. "It's more a case of reaping the rewards of my sins."

"I don't understand."

"Steroids," he said simply. "My doctor says he's never seen a case quite like mine, but the theory is anabolic steroids plus genetics plus the physical abuse inherent to playing a contact sport is what led to the condition. Definitely not my smartest move."

She nodded as though she really understood. "That goes along with one of my favorite sayings. Do you know what results in good judgment?" When he shook his head, she said, "Experience."

He grinned. "If that's not the truth…"

"And what results in experience?" She paused for a beat.

"Poor judgment," he guessed, then grinned more widely when she nodded. "I have to remember that. I like it." He threw the Frisbees once more. "Anyway, surgery last January wasn't successful, and medications haven't helped, either. The docs tell me that's the way it is sometimes. Too much irreversible damage, and nothing can be done."

"How much vision do you have left?" she asked.

He made a circle with his thumb and forefinger that was about four inches in diameter, and held it in front of his eyes. "Everything on the outside of that circle is black. My doc says it might stabilize and stay like this for a while, or the rest of the field of vision might close and be gone in a matter of days."

"So you're praying for a miracle now." She said it as though she was teasing.

"Nope," Brian said, turning slightly, so he could see her, comparing the circle of his vision to what he remembered from the previous day. "That would be taking away my responsibility for what I did to myself."

Her smile faded to a softer expression, as though she once more understood exactly what he meant.

He noticed immediately. "You know?" he added, enjoying the connection with her. Especially because she hadn't offered him any of the heartfelt—and unhelpful—sympathy or platitudes that others had.

"Oh, that." She rolled her eyes and grinned. "I've been there more than once myself."

"To the point you royally screwed up your life?"

He'd meant the question to be a rhetorical one so he was surprised when she nodded.

"Hard to believe. You look—"

"Looks can be deceiving," she said, her smile fading. "Let's just say that I've too much experience—" the smile came back, rueful and directed at herself "—you know, that thing leading to good judgment—and plenty of practice with the Serenity Prayer."

Though he was curious, he didn't ask about the circumstances. But he wanted to. He liked her. In their all-too-brief meetings, all those reasons for not getting involved lost importance.

"That matter-of-fact way you talk about being responsible for your own stuff," she added when he caught her glance, "you'd be surprised at how rare that is."

He grinned at how neatly she had turned the sub-

ject away from herself. His own lack of responsibility
had been a point of contention between him and his
grandfather for years. Brian was trying hard to rectify
that, so her observation pleased him. "Maybe the world
wouldn't be in such a mess if more people did."

Even more, he liked that she hadn't turned all clini-
cal on him about how little he saw. One more thing that
made her easy to be around, made him aware of her as
a woman. Too aware. Once more, he reminded himself
this wasn't the time to get involved with anyone.

"Tell me about your foundation." She threw the
tennis ball for a couple of the dogs, grinning as the
big sissy-looking poodle in the red sweater flew into
the air to catch one. "Why is it named the Beanstalk
Gang?"

"Because it was my favorite story when I was a boy,"
Brian said. "I think we're all given the equivalent of
magic beans somewhere along the way in the form of
opportunities—which are usually disguised as hard
work—or advantages, like a talent to sing or play ball
or be great with a computer. It's what we do with those
things that counts. But, the story is also cautionary. Jack
followed a calling by climbing up the beanstalk, but he
also caused himself a lot of trouble by stealing from
the giant. I think it's a reminder that kids have to learn
responsibility and let go of thinking they're entitled to
anything. My grandfather always told me that for every
privilege there's an equal responsibility."

"The work you do there…you sound like you love it."

"It's what I'm supposed to be doing," he said simply,
meaning it. At one point, he hadn't been able to imagine

his life after football. Then a high school buddy who was now a teacher had told him about all the trouble the school had begun having with gang violence and vandalism, something he traced back to the suspension of after-school programs after funding was cut. That conversation had sparked Brian's imagination, and when he'd realized that he had the money—and fund-raising ability—to do something about the situation, he'd thrown himself into the project, more satisfied with the charity work than he'd been about anything else in his life. Making such a confession to anyone, though, made him sound like some self-righteous do-gooder, and that wasn't the case at all.

The newspaper article that had been in the paper last week was mostly accurate, a nice change for him, and it had done exactly what he had hoped in raising awareness—and money. The foundation website had received ten times the number of hits since the article, and the donations had gone way up.

He turned his head to look at Angela, not knowing what else to say that wouldn't make him sound like some self-aggrandizing celebrity calling attention to himself.

"I feel that way about training service dogs," she said.

The fact that she didn't pry a bit surprised him. Pleased him.

They didn't talk for a couple of minutes while they continued to play catch and fetch with the dogs. Angela was good company, quite unlike the women he used to spend time with. He had liked girls with flash, second only to playing football. When he was younger, the key to success with both sports and girls was being bigger, stronger than the other guys. He'd known taking steroids was wrong, but at the time he'd had the misguided idea that the end justified the means. Twenty years later, he was paying the price.

Forcing his attention away from those gloomy thoughts to the dogs playing in front of them, he sized up each one. The poodle in the sweater kept coming into his line of vision, and Brian decided it was a good thing the dog was wearing a sweater. Otherwise, he would have looked like a seventy-pound rat. The most alluring dog of the group was Polly, the dog he had met yesterday, even though he knew she was being trained to help someone else. He also really liked the golden retriever and the Lab mix.

With effort, he returned his thoughts to the topic Angela had started. "The work of the foundation—that's the thing that drives me," he finally said. "I have a few months left before most of my vision is gone if I'm lucky, days if I'm not. In the meantime, I want to get as much set up as I can." He looked around at the dogs, able to imagine all of them except the poodle as his guide dog. "Is there a chance I could have one of these dogs?"

She nodded, a smile making her eyes light. "Polly, Bailey and Checkers are being trained for hearing-impaired owners. Gatsby and Jasper are being trained for the blind. Gatsby is already spoken for."

"That leaves Jasper," he said.

"It does. Why don't you call him?"

Brian did, and the prissy poodle in the red sweater came to sit in front of him.

THREE

"He has purple hair," Brian said, looking at the dog, who stared right back at him with dark, intelligent eyes. He had the fleeting impression that the dog was sizing him up—and that he might come up lacking.

"Disgusting, isn't it," Angela agreed cheerfully. "He just had a haircut, so most of it is gone. You should have seen him when he first got here. A full continental cut and purple from his head to the pom-pom on his tail."

"So he'll be white when the last of this is cut off?"

"Yes. His previous owner thought he was a fashion accessory, not a dog." Angela came to stand next to Brian, the top of her head just at his shoulder. "Imagine how humiliating it would be to be dyed purple so you go with an outfit, then taken to a function where you're supposed to act like a stuffed dog."

"Sounds bad."

The dog appeared to wink, which made Brian grin, though he still couldn't believe that Angela saw him with this particular dog.

"It gets worse," Angela assured him. "This was an outdoor affair, a fashion show. There was a close-by bolt of lightning and a huge crack of thunder. Jasper's owner screamed and dropped his leash. Rain started falling in buckets, and Jasper, exercising good sense, headed for the nearest shelter—the buffet table."

"That couldn't have been good."

"It wasn't," Angela said, glancing at him. "The hero of our sad tale—"

Unable to resist, Brian teased, "Would that be tail with an *i* or—"

Grinning, Angela nudged him with her elbow. "Be good."

"The buffet table," Brian prompted, imagining the event. White tablecloths and a gallery of who's who all dressed in their *Vogue* and *GQ* finest.

"Jasper caught the tablecloth in his crown." Catching his glance once more, Angela held up a hand. "Don't ask me why he was wearing a crown. I don't know. But when everyone started shouting, he ran. Or tried to."

Jasper winked again, and Brian patted the top of his head.

"Evidently embarrassment and being expected to pay for thousands of dollars of seafood delicacies were too much for his owner. She had him taken to the pound with orders that he be put down."

"You're kidding." Brian's heart fell, the story going from funny to heartbreaking in an instant. He admitted the story put the dog in a different league. He still couldn't imagine Jasper as the dog for him. "How do you know all this?"

"A friend who was there told me about it. In fact, she was the one who told me he was in the pound. Unfortunately, it took us almost six weeks to get him out. He's been here five months now."

Brian felt sympathy for the dog and couldn't resist scratching his ears, the fur surprisingly soft.

"He's the smartest dog I've ever worked with," Angela continued.

"You should be the star of your own show," Brian said to the dog. "For putting up with bad hair days and people who don't understand." He glanced at Angela. "I'm sure he's great, but I don't quite see myself with a poodle."

"He's an athlete," she countered. "He'd go jogging with you."

How could she know jogging was important to him and that he'd been wondering how he could continue after his sight was gone? "I think a golden retriever or a German shepherd—"

"Did you know that poodles were originally used for hunting?" She waited until Brian looked from the dog to her. "Or that in Russia they were used to haul milk carts? These dogs were first bred to be working dogs. He may look fragile, but he's not."

"Can I think about it?"

"Of course." She looked away, then back at him. "This whole process of having you involved in the training is unorthodox and unproven. Decades of experience from other training facilities have owners coming to the dogs only after they've completed their training. Bottom line, there's a good chance this might not work."

"You're not going to talk me out of this," Brian said, "even if I'm not sure the poodle is the right dog for me."

"From the beginning of the process to turning over a fully trained dog is a huge investment of time and effort. The dogs that are specifically bred for use as guide dogs are earmarked for the training facilities they are contracted with. It could be a long time before I have access to another dog who is as good as Jasper." When she met his gaze, her beautiful eyes were serious.

"I understand." Brian stared down at her, liking her conviction and her passion for her work. She was close enough he didn't have to compensate for his peripheral vision being completely gone. This close, he could see a fine blue vein beneath her skin at her temple and varying shades of brown in her luminous eyes. She stared back at him, the attraction shimmering between them. With effort, he reclaimed the thread of what he needed to say to her. "Whatever releases you need that absolve you from any liability, I'll sign them."

She waved a hand. "I wasn't thinking about that." She looked back at Jasper. "I was thinking about the dog. You have weeks to months before your vision is…"

"Gone?" Brian finally prompted.

"An uncertain amount of time," she qualified. "For every guide dog we've trained, we've assessed dozens that didn't make the grade." She met his gaze square on, all businesslike again, making him wonder if he had imagined that instant of mutual interest.

"So the poodle is the dog you think I should have?"

"His name is Jasper. And yes, he'd be a good dog for you."

"Are you always this blunt?"

She looked away for a moment, and surprised him

once more by smiling when she turned back to him. "When it comes to the dogs, yes."

The storm door at the back of the house slammed, drawing Brian's attention. When he looked toward the sound, he became acutely aware once more of just how much his field of vision had shrunk in the past month, reminding him that he didn't have a lot of time left before his sight was gone completely.

"Angela," Maisey called, coming toward them.

She wasn't alone. The guy Angela had been talking to yesterday was with her, a smug smile on his face as he strolled along, his hands in his pockets. Angela was in the fog that had once been Brian's peripheral vision, so he had to turn his head until he could see her. There was a glint of anger in her eyes.

Interesting. It wasn't the look of a woman happy to see a boyfriend, and yesterday Brian had been sure that's exactly who this guy was. Something eased in his chest, a feeling of joy he hadn't even been aware of. In that split second he realized his interest in Angela went beyond the simple appreciation of an alluring and intriguing woman ... and the timing couldn't have been worse.

"I told you yesterday that I didn't want to see you again," Angela said, focusing on the man.

Maisey's smile vanished as she came to a halt. "Who are you?"

"This—" Angela took a breath, waving a hand "—is Tommy Manderoll."

"Oh." Maisey turned an accusing look on Tommy. "You're the one who left all those messages."

Brian wondered at the wealth of meaning in Maisey's voice as she put her hands on her waist and leveled a schoolteacher's frown at Tommy.

Angela's gaze went from Tommy to Maisey, then met Brian's. Her expression was neutral enough, but the furious glint was still there. "Excuse me a moment," she said to him. "Maisey, maybe you could talk to Brian a little about our training protocols."

"Sure."

Angela pointed a finger at Tommy. "You come with me."

He grinned. "Just what I was hoping for."

Shaking with annoyance, Angela headed toward the office, contemplating how to best get rid of him. She didn't want him coming around, didn't want him involved in her life in any way at all. She mentally counted to ten, reminding herself of her life now, her happiness, and her personal determination to live up to Maisey's and Reverend Chester's faith in her—and her newfound faith in herself.

She stopped a few feet away from the door and turned on Tommy, hating the twisting knots of old, familiar, hated cravings that threatened everything.

"I was very clear yesterday," she said. "I don't want *anything* to do with you. Whatever you're involved with, I don't want any part of it."

"You weren't always so uptight."

She made a shooing motion toward the parking lot at the side of the house. "Just go or I'll call the po—"

"Who?" he taunted. "The police? I don't think so." He folded his fingers against his palm, then fanned them out like a magician, a small white packet appearing between his fingers. "I have what you want."

She recognized what it was, and her heart lurched. Just the sight of it made her nerves dance. One part of her longed to reach for the cocaine even as memory after memory washed over her at the terrible things she had done in exchange for those fleeting moments of euphoria. Her mouth dried as she wiped her suddenly sweaty palms against her jeans.

"You know it." He smiled, drawing her attention back to his face. "And I know it."

"Go away, Tommy." Her voice was pleading instead of commanding, and she hated herself for it.

He looked toward the yard, and Angela followed his gaze. Brian was smiling at something Maisey had said, Maisey's posture animated the way it got when she talked about training dogs. The woman meant everything to Angela, as much as Reverend Chester and her life-long friend, Rachel McLeod. Angela looked back at Tommy, a living reminder of the mountain of regret she felt for the dreadful things she had done.

"Take your drugs and your innuendos and go." She was proud of the firm tone in her voice. "As for calling the police, you can bet I will."

"This is me you're talking to, doll face." Tommy waved toward the dogs. "Don't make threats you'll never follow up on. Do you honestly think a convicted felon can withstand the kind of scrutiny that will come your way? It's one thing to talk to a chamber of commerce and solicit a few puny donations for a good cause. But what about when a reporter comes around and does an in-depth story and discovers the truth about you?" He nodded toward Brian. "He's here to donate to your little charity, I bet."

"What if he is?" she challenged, thankful Tommy didn't know the real reason behind Brian's visit.

"I'll make you a deal, and before you go shaking your head at me, you might want to know the terms."

"There's nothing you can possibly say—"

"Maybe you put the half million dollars into this business, so you're a little short of cash—that means you have equity and you can get it. I need a stake—"

"A patsy," Angela said, remembering that he had somehow convinced her to take out a loan against Victorian Rose Antiques, the business she and her best friend, Rachel, had owned. Angela rationalized that she hadn't known until later he had used the money to buy a kilo of cocaine…but deep in her heart she had, and she'd had the drug-induced conviction that she could make everything work out. She'd been wrong.

"And you have the money—don't even bother denying it because I don't believe you." He glanced toward Maisey and Brian, then back at her. "Get it, and I won't dig up every piece of dirt that I can find on your famous new boyfriend. You know how the media just loves a juicy story." He motioned as though reading a headline. "The Football Player and the Felon." Tommy pressed the small packet into the pocket of her denim shirt. "Something to help you think."

He turned away then, walking around the side of the house toward his car with that I-own-the-world bounce in his step. In her pocket, the packet of cocaine—she knew that's what it was, could smell it though it had no discernible odor—whispered seductively to her.

She looked back toward Brian and Maisey. He was listening attentively, his fingers absently petting Jasper each time the dog butted his head against his palm. Angela watched them a moment longer, then went into the office where she sat down at her desk, despair wrapping its claws around her throat. She took the packet out of her pocket, her thoughts chaotic, her fingers trembling.

With the bottomless pit where she'd once been firmly in mind, she marched into the bathroom and flushed the packet down the toilet. Then she washed her hands, feeling as dirty as she had the day she was arrested.

Going back into the office, she sat down at the desk, placing her hands flat on the blotter. To her dismay, they were trembling.

With that, she picked up the receiver of the phone and dialed the number of her lifeline. "It's me, Angela," she said after the familiar voice of Reverend Chester Holt said hello.

"How are you?" he asked.

Relief washed over her, and she sank back into the chair. "I'm good." He wouldn't let her get away with that for long, she knew, but for now just having the conversation with the man who'd been more like a father to her was enough. "I just wanted to hear your voice. How are Sarah and Andy—growing, I bet. And Rachel—"

"Hungry for news, are you?" he said around a laugh.

"You know it."

Wrapping the receiver cord around her finger, she felt the tension fall away while Reverend Holt told her about Sarah's and Andy's latest escapades and about the big celebration they'd had when Rachel's new husband, Micah, adopted them. They were all happy and doing well. For that, Angela was thankful. She and Rachel still weren't speaking, and Angela couldn't blame her. Still, she longed to make up with her old friend, wanted it with all her heart, and knew that even though she had tried before, she hadn't tried hard enough. The next step was up to her.

Despite the rift between herself and Rachel, Reverend Chester had remained steadfast, visiting her every couple of weeks while she had been in prison, and providing guidance that had helped her grow into the person she was meant to be.

"Now tell me about you," Reverend Chester said.

"I'm fine."

"Angela, girl, that's the answer you give this old man when you're anything but fine."

That fast, the tension was back.

"The truth…" Her voice trailed away, and she dropped her head, tucking the receiver between her neck and chin, pressing her fingers against her eyes.

The silence stretched painfully, and she knew he'd wait with all the patience in the world without saying a word until she did.

"I'm scared, Rev," she whispered.

"Ah," he said, his voice comforting with that single word. "Your faith is a little shaky today, is it?"

"Yes."

"Tell me about the dogs," he said.

The abrupt change in topic was usual for him, and

she'd been through the process often enough to know that she'd be rewarded with some insight. She focused her narrative on Checkers, who would soon go home with deaf, eighty-year-old Greg Proudie. The man's wife had died about a year ago and his son had introduced the idea of a service dog. The dog was a perfect fit for Proudie, and Angela was proud of the work they had done.

"He's going to be great with his new owner," she concluded, "who is participating in the last of his training."

"How do you know he's going to be great?" Reverend Chester asked.

"I just know—"

"You have faith."

"Of course."

"No fear?"

"Fear?" So there was the point he wanted to make. Her gaze went to the window where sunlight streamed in.

"Faith is harder to keep in focus when you're afraid," he said. "Faith is knowing, the way you know the dog you're telling me about will do well. Fear is letting the unknown consume you." He paused. "And you know the pathway to faith, Angela."

"Prayer," she breathed. He was right, of course. An obvious reminder she needed.

"That's right. And you know you're in mine."

The door to the training yard opened accompanied by Brian's and Maisey's voices.

"Thanks for taking the time to talk," Angela said,

looking toward the hallway where they were walking toward her. "I have my bearings back."

"You hadn't really lost them," Reverend Chester said. "Stay in touch."

Angela said goodbye and disconnected the call.

"Here you are," Maisey said after Angela hung up the phone. "You got rid of that Tommy person?"

"For now." Angela suspected he would be back, just like the bad penny he was. She had to figure out what to do about that.

"Brian has decided to follow your recommendation about Jasper and wants to know when you guys can get started." Maisey looked from her to Brian. "And I told him right away."

Good news…if it weren't for Tommy's threat to dig up dirt on Brian. And since Brian had confessed to her about reaping the rewards of his sins, she had the feeling working with him would be opening up Pandora's box. But since she'd already agreed, how could she turn him away?

FOUR

Hours later, Angela came through the back door to their offices, and Maisey called to her. Following the sound of voices, Angela found Maisey in the front room, her face lit with her usual beaming smile when she talked about Guardian Paws. "Angela, this nice young man is Andrew Brogg. He's a reporter with the *Denver Chronicle*, and also a part-time correspondent for Channel 7."

Angela recognized the journalist's name from the investigative pieces he did, the latest one accusing a university president of using public money to finance improvements on his home.

"After all the things Ms. Erdmann told me about you," he said, extending his hand, "I was expecting you to be about ten feet tall." Behind wire-rimmed glasses, calculating brown eyes met her own. He smiled. "It's nice to meet you."

"Thanks," Angela responded. Since he had made a reputation for himself on scandals associated with various local and regional entities, having him show up on the same day as Tommy put her on alert.

Reporters had a way of twisting things to meet their own agenda, no matter how charming they might appear. She'd had her own up-close-and-personal experience, and she'd learned one important lesson—never take any reporter at face value.

"He wants to do a feature article on Guardian Paws," Maisey said.

"What kind of feature could be interesting to you?" Angela wondered if he worked hard to look exactly like a stereotypical newspaper reporter. He wore a shapeless corduroy sports coat, plaid shirt and scuffed athletic shoes. A black nylon briefcase hung over his shoulder, and in his hand was a stenographer's notebook and pen. "I've read some of your stories, Mr. Brogg. Like the ones you did on the stockyards near Greeley and a toxic spill at Rocky Flats. I can't imagine a man of your talents being interested in what we do."

"It's nice to meet someone who remembers my work," he said.

"Really, there's no great exposé here," she added. The Guardian Paws Web site had a link to the prison program where she had learned to train dogs, and when she was asked about it, she told her story. So her prison record wasn't a secret. "So I can't imagine what might be of interest to you."

He smiled again. "It's the season. You know, peace on earth and feel-good stories." He turned toward Maisey. "If we could focus in on a child—say one in a wheelchair—with a dog to the rescue. What's not to love?"

His explanation was as cynical a one as Angela had

heard about Christmas in a long time. "I think you misunderstand the nature of our work," she said.

"Then enlighten me. Let me interview you." Once more his gaze went from her to Maisey as if he thought she was the softer target, his expression conveying nothing but earnest appeal. "I'm not planning an exposé. Just a human interest story for my readers about two women making a difference in their community."

Angela heard the word *planning,* and for the moment, she couldn't decide if that seemingly careful choice was her own imagination or him being cagey. If his story turned out to be something else, he had himself covered. Too easily she imagined him telling her that he'd simply followed the story where it took him if it happened to turn into an exposé. Given her history, that's exactly what she expected rather than one about a woman taking full advantage of her second chance and turning her life around.

"See?" Maisey beamed. "A feel-good story. Maybe one of our clients would agree to be featured. And if it brings in some donations, think of the additional things we could do."

Though her business partner was right about that, they weren't that short of money. They had recently received a grant that provided funding to cover expenses for the next year, and donations had been steadily coming in.

"Maisey tells me you do the majority of the training," Andrew said to Angela, as though everything was all decided. And, in a way, it was. Given the tone of the couple of stories that Angela had read, she assumed they'd be piquing his curiosity if they turned him down. The goal now was to figure out how to defuse his interest—especially since she didn't believe his agenda.

"So," he continued, "I'd like to begin by interviewing you." He looked poised to open his notebook.

No way was she going to do that until she'd had a chance to really think through what to say to him. "I need to check my schedule," she said.

"Fine." He inclined his head toward the desk visible through the open doorway.

Feeling cornered and not seeing any rescue from Maisey, Angela headed toward the desk and pulled out her appointment book. "How about next Tuesday at four?"

"That's Thanksgiving week," he countered, openly looking over her shoulder and reading the entries. "I'd really like to get a jump on this before then." He pointed to the following evening's date. "How about tomorrow at six-thirty, and you can tell me about things over dinner?"

Angela looked up at Maisey, who watched her with a smile on her face and puzzlement in her eyes.

"Okay." Angela made a notation in the appointment book, then closed it. "Where would you like to meet?"

"How about the Larimer Grill just off the Sixteenth Street Mall?" he said. "The food is good and it's convenient."

Convenient? Angela thought. Only if you worked downtown. So, not only would she have to have dinner with a man she didn't want to talk to, she now had to navigate through Denver's rush-hour traffic to get there.

Suppressing a sigh, she said, "I'll see you then."

"Great," Andrew said, then said his goodbyes and headed for his vehicle. People were normally cooperative unless they had closets they didn't want him poking through.

He knew Angela London's type—the casual ones who played everything low-key and always had big skeletons rattling in the closet. When he reached his car, he punched the speed dial for the editorial assistant assigned to his department. "Find out everything you can about Angela London," he said. "Approximate age is thirty-five."

"Just a quick search?" the assistant asked. "Or the works?"

"The works," Andrew said, still puzzled as to why Ramsey had come here. "I want to know everything about this woman. Where she went to school, where she's worked, who her friends are and what she eats for breakfast." He mostly wanted to know what her connection to Brian Ramsey was, especially since her appointment book had his name written down for more than half the days over the next week.

The relationship couldn't be personal—she wasn't Brian Ramsey's type, not if his socialite ex-fiancée was any indication. Andrew had contacted the woman, and, following up on the rumors peppered through his thick file, he'd asked her point-blank about Brian's use of steroids. She had flushed and stammered before telling him to talk to Brian. Andrew hadn't found the supplier yet, but he would. It was just a case of poking around in the right closet. Maybe Angela London's.

Unrelated pieces of information were coming together, and Andrew could smell the story. Ramsey's
sudden, premature retirement from football just before training camp opened last summer. A fiancée
who bailed mere weeks before the wedding. A kid involved with the Beanstalk Gang, Ramsey's foundation,
arrested for trying to sell drugs to an undercover cop,
a case where the charges were dropped and everything
was hushed up. Andrew could sense a cover-up, especially since he hadn't been able to get close enough to
Ramsey to ask a single question. It was time to call the
man again.

Andrew didn't know how all the pieces fit yet, nor
did he know how Angela London fit into it. But he
would. Anything to do with celebrities and their falls
from grace was a sure bet. For once, Andrew was going
to be positioned to cash in. He had floated a book idea
to a publisher, promising a lurid tell-all. Andrew was
sick of the celebrity athletes who thought they could get
away with things that would have landed him in jail.
And he had no doubt Brian Ramsey was one of them,
getting away with who knew what while pretending to
be a white knight.

Andrew intended to prove it.

"You're in one of those tabloids again," Gramps said
to Brian when he arrived home an hour after leaving
Guardian Paws. Brian turned his head so he could look
at his grandfather, who was perched on a stool next to
the counter and who remained absorbed in the paper
in front of him.

"It says right here that Erica left you because you gambled away all your money," Gramps added, poking the paper.

"You know me better than that. I don't gamble." Brian walked around the island in the center of the kitchen where his grandmother stood, putting the finishing touches on a pie that was about to go into the oven. Even though the cook would be in to make the evening meal, Nonnie still baked, and her pies were the best. "How was your day?" he asked, dropping a kiss on her cheek. "I hope that's apple."

"It is," she said. "And my day was just fine until this old fool started talking about the latest story in that old rag. Tell him that it's not true."

"It's not true," Brian said.

"Humph," Gramps said. "Don't know why they'd be printing stuff that wasn't. A newspaper has a responsibility. Report facts and only the facts. How can they get away with this?" He looked up at Brian as though he expected an answer even though they'd had the same discussion dozens of times.

"They're counting on me not to sue them," he replied, heading for the stairwell to the second floor.

"Well, if it isn't true, you ought to. It says right here that you're depressed over your retirement from football and that you're suicidal."

"It's fiction," Brian said. "I'm fine. Ignore it."

He put his foot down on the first step, somehow missed it, and stumbled before completely losing his balance and hitting the floor.

Irritated and humiliated, Brian lifted his head and

sat up while Nonnie said, "Oh, my goodness. Are you okay?"

In the next second, Gramps was looming above him with his hands on his hips. "Don't coddle the boy. If nothing's broken, get on your feet."

"Just give him a minute," Nonnie said, leaning over and coming into his line of vision.

She had that same look of concern on her face that she'd had ever since Brian had told them that he was losing his sight. He managed a smile that hid his irritation with himself. "I'm fine." That phrase was getting to be old, he thought as he stood.

I'm fine—there's nothing to worry about…if you don't include the fact that I'm scared spitless.

"Really," he added. He turned his head, taking in his grandparents. Nonnie gave him an encouraging smile when he looked at her, and Gramps did his usual glower. "I'm going to change my clothes, then go work out for an hour."

Once more he headed for the stairwell, this time grabbing the banister before putting his foot on the first step.

"You're too hard on him," he heard Nonnie say as he went up the stairs.

"Not hard enough," Gramps replied.

Nothing new in that conversation, Brian thought as he reached the top of the stairs, making sure that he turned his head so he could see the doorway at the end of the wide hallway. Since the day he had arrived in their home when he was six years old, Gramps had been saying basically the same thing. Every day since then, Brian felt as though he hadn't measured up and as though his grandfather expected him to be as big a screwup as his mother had been. He knew the story because Gramps had repeated it often.

She had been a party girl who liked the fast life—fast boys, fast cars, fast times made even more so by her drug use. The last time Brian had seen her, she'd been strung out on crack. He hadn't needed his grandfather's warning to make a vow that he'd never use, never be involved in that life in any way at all. He didn't want that for himself, and he didn't want anything to do with people who were part of that life. Somehow, though, his Gramps kept expecting that the sins of his mother would become his, as well.

Brian's wish now was pretty much the same as it had been then—find a way to make his grandfather proud of him.

Brian pushed open the double doors that led to his suite just as the BlackBerry in his pocket began ringing.

"Ramsey here," he said.

"Brian, it's Dwight" came his manager's voice through the receiver. "How are you?"

"Fine." That again.

"I just wanted to let you know we have things all set to shoot the last commercial for your sponsor. I just emailed you the information."

"When and where?" At last, Brian thought, some good news. Finishing his endorsement contract with the National Milk Association was one of the things he most wanted before the holidays began.

The minute the final commercial was accepted, he

needed to break the news to them about the reasons for his sight loss. Since there was a strict morals clause in the contract related to drug abuse, they needed to hear the sorry truth from him rather than it coming through a tabloid story. Though he'd been clean for years when he had signed the contract, he'd had a change of heart in thinking his previous behavior hadn't mattered. It did, and he didn't want any negative fallout to come near them even though his attorney and manager had both advised against making any confessions until after all the terms were fulfilled. His attorney assured him that he was legally in the clear. Maybe. But Brian didn't feel morally in the clear.

"The ad company is working on a hometown angle," Dwight said, interrupting Brian's morose thoughts. "So you don't have to travel."

"More good news,"

"I set it up for Monday and Tuesday of next week since I figured you might be traveling on Wednesday."

"Where would I go?" Brian asked, pressing the speaker button on the BlackBerry so he could continue to talk to Dwight while he punched in the button for the calendar to see if he had appointments he'd forgotten about. He squinted at the display, which looked fuzzy to him. He looked away, then back, the display coming into focus. No appointments on Wednesday.

"Aspen," Dwight drawled. "It's Thanksgiving, and I thought that's where you always said you'd spend Thanksgiving after you retired."

He was surprised that Dwight remembered. Thanksgiving in Aspen had been Erica's dream, though. Not his. "No, I'll be right here."

This was the first Thanksgiving in years that wouldn't be spent in practice or as a game day. And the date had arrived unnoticed. He wondered if his grandparents had planned anything. He hadn't eaten Thanksgiving dinner with them in years.

"I'll call you back in the morning as soon as I have times nailed down," George said.

"I'll talk to you then," Brian said, disconnecting the call and slipping the phone into his pocket. He crossed the room so he could look through the window at the view of Mount Evans, taking in everything he could about this vista. The shape of the peak and surrounding Front Range ramparts. The brilliant hue of everything the sun touched.

Sighing, he turned away to take in the sitting room and his bedroom beyond. The purchase of this home that provided the kind of luxuries he'd always imagined having should have been the culmination of a dream. Instead, he felt cheated.

Once, he would have kicked off his shoes and left them lying on the floor as he crossed the sitting room. He didn't take them off until he had gone through the bedroom and into the closet. He put them on the rack next to the others, then sat on the stool in the middle of the room, propped his elbows on his knees and rested his head against his hands.

"You're fine," he repeated to himself. "Like Gramps says, life isn't a game for sissies."

Here, though, in the closet of his million-dollar

house, he admitted what he wouldn't to anyone else, anywhere else. He wanted a replay. He wanted back his career and the familiar life of being an athlete at the top of his game. He wanted his fiancée back and the life he'd thought they would have after they were married. He wanted her to take back the words she'd said when she canceled the wedding.

"You're handicapped, and that's not the man I fell in love with. Maybe some women can deal with that, but I know myself." And Erica had kissed him, then turned to leave him forever. "I'd hate you, Brian, and I don't want to live like that."

He had hated her for a while. Now...now he was simply tired.

And he couldn't admit to anyone that he was haunted by an image from his childhood of a blind beggar who had hung out at the corner of Colfax and Washington. In Brian's nightmares, he was that man.

Raising his head, he looked around the closet that was far bigger than the bedroom he'd had as a child, where clothes hung in neat precision because a maid came in every day and cleaned up after him.

"I'm fine," he whispered. Then he changed into workout gear and went back downstairs. He took the stairs at the front of the house this time, which curved around a large foyer. The wide, oval foyer had space for the baby grand that Brian had purchased for his grandmother. The piano was artfully tucked beneath the stairs, per a designer's suggestion, along with a pair of settees.

Brian went through another door and down another

flight of stairs, once more comparing the small circle of his vision from what he remembered yesterday. Not smaller than yesterday, but definitely smaller than a week ago.

He pushed open the doors to the training room. Brilliant light poured through the west-facing windows. In the distance, the sun was sliding behind Mount Evans. He'd wanted to be alone, but Sam was at the Bowflex.

"I thought you weren't going to work out tonight," Sam said.

"Changed my mind." Brian headed for the bench where he began his warm-up routine. "Thought you were headed home to get ready for a date."

"That's not for a couple of hours, so I decided to work out first." Something of Brian's mood must have been evident because Sam added, "I can leave if you want to be alone."

"I'm fine."

Fine. Brian decided he really disliked that word.

They were both quiet for a couple of minutes. Usually his mind settled and his thoughts stopped swirling as he went through his exercises. Today, an endless list paraded through his mind.

"Plan the work. Work the plan," he muttered.

"That's what you always say," Sam agreed from across the room. He'd moved to the incline bench were he was working through a series of curls. "I checked tomorrow's schedule. It's open except for your appointment with Angela in the morning. Anything unexpected come up?"

Brian shook his head. "Not yet." In fact, he prayed there'd be nothing unexpected.

"Andrew Brogg called me again this afternoon," Sam said.

Prayed. Like that ever worked. The reporter had been circling the last few months like a vulture, so hearing his name wasn't unexpected, just unpleasant.

Brian looked at Sam, who was now working through his cool-down exercises. A month ago, they'd had a conversation about keeping control of things. As clearly as though he was speaking right now, Brian heard Sam's voice in his head. "Just a thought, buddy, but you might think about turning this over to a Higher Power." And just as clearly, he heard his own response. "No offense, but that's always sounded like a cop-out." At the moment, though, it sounded good. Turning his problems over to someone else, something else. Someone who had a better plan than he did.

Sam reached for a towel and wiped his face before hanging it around his neck. "He said to ask you if the name Val Fitzwater meant anything to you."

Unfortunately, Brian knew the name well. The man had been his primary supplier for steroids a decade earlier.

The vulture was closing in, and Brian had no idea how to stop it.

FIVE

"You're not trusting Jasper to guide you," Angela said to Brian the following day after he tried to prevent the dog from walking off the sidewalk. "Let's stop a minute."

"What am I missing, coach?" Angela had laughed the first time he'd called her that a couple of hours ago, so he'd kept it up. It was also an intentional reminder to himself of the relationship he was trying hard to maintain. She was his coach for the duration—that was *all* she could be.

They had been walking through one of the older neighborhoods in Brighton. It had once been a small farming town and was now a suburb on Denver's northeast side. She liked this area, she'd told him, because there was a good mix between residential and business all within a few blocks—a perfect environment for training a guide dog. And the town was only a couple of miles from Guardian Paws.

He'd expected learning to walk with the dog would be the easiest of all the things he had to learn for his new sightless life. Jasper clearly had an excellent grasp of thirty or so commands in addition to his other skills, but Brian was having trouble keeping them all straight. These were the basics and should be no more difficult than practicing dropback drills.

"Raise your arm," she commanded.

He did and immediately felt a branch that was no more than an inch or two above his head. "So that's why he decided to take me off the sidewalk."

"That's right," Angela agreed. "Since you've given him mixed messages, it's important to praise him so his good behavior is reinforced."

"Good boy, Jasper." He touched the dog's head where the soft wiry hair no longer surprised him as it first had. She was right, of course. He didn't yet trust Jasper, though he liked him more and more each time they were together.

Brian turned his head to look at Angela. She stood no more than three feet away and her face was all he could see. The field of vision was quite a lot smaller than a few days ago. Like a thief, the glaucoma was stealing his sighted time. Though he'd done his best to convince himself and everyone around him that he was dealing with this, he wasn't ready to admit to anyone that his sight was rapidly deteriorating.

"Ready to go?" she asked.

"Forward," he commanded Jasper, doing his best to keep his tension from radiating through the harness, another thing that Angela had cautioned him about.

They took off once more at a brisk pace. Rather than trying to anticipate the dog's movements as he had been doing, Brian closed his eyes and let the dog lead. He wanted to try and ignore the fact that it wasn't that much darker with his eyes closed than it was with them open.

That simple act, though, made him more aware of his surroundings. Next to him, he could feel Angela's presence, mostly in the faint feminine fragrance he'd come to associate with her. He heard the loud thrum of the bass from a car stereo a block or so away. Against his face and hands, the air was cold and carried the smell of the local stockyards.

"It could snow later," he said.

"What makes you say so?"

"When the weather's infamous upslope develops before a snow storm, it always brings in the smell of the stockyards east of here."

She chuckled, just as he had hoped she would. "I'll have to pay more attention."

"See, my superpowers of perception are kicking in." Not true, but once more she laughed just as he wanted. The point was to diffuse his own worry that continually squeezed his chest the way it had the first months after his mother had abandoned him. That fast, the worry was back.

"Do you ever worry, coach?" he asked.

She laughed once more. "All the time, but not about this part. You're doing fine, you know."

"I feel like a rookie stepping onto the field for his first game. Like I haven't mastered the basics, and I'll never figure them out."

"And that feeling went away when?"

This time he chuckled. "It came back before every game and left after the first snap."

She was quiet a moment. "And then you're too busy to worry? You're just playing?"

"That's right."

"I don't know enough about the game to give you any concrete comparisons, but I'm sure this is like learning anything new. Certain skills have to be mastered, and once you do, they become second nature so you don't think about them." She was quiet a moment while they continued walking, then she added, "Maybe you're not quite ready for the varsity squad, but you're doing fine."

"That sounds like a challenge," he returned.

"I have the feeling you've been successfully rising to those your whole life."

They fell silent while he filed away her matter-of-fact statement to appreciate later. His focus came back to Jasper, who was once more steering him off the middle of the sidewalk. This time Brian followed.

"What's your dog's name?"

At the sound of the child's voice, Brian started.

So that was the obstacle, and he hadn't seen it. He bent his head toward the sound, and there in the middle of the walk was a boy bundled in a coat and bright red mittens, sitting on a tricycle.

"Jasper," Brian replied. "What's yours?"

"I'm not supposed to talk to strangers," the kid said, ignoring the fact that he was the one who had started the conversation.

Brian laughed. "Good advice, kid."

"How are you today?" another voice called, this one feminine.

"Fine," Angela called back. "It has sure gotten cold over the last hour, though."

Once more, Brian turned toward the voice, his gaze finally finding the shadowy image of a woman on the porch of the house they were passing.

"The poodle is looking good," the woman said.

"He's about to graduate," Angela returned, pride in her voice.

"So maybe we'll be seeing more poodles as guide dogs?" the woman said.

"I hope so."

They walked another half block, then Brian asked, "You must be a familiar sight around here."

"Pretty much, since I'm up and down these streets almost every day."

He realized he was hearing more traffic sounds. "We've got to be getting close to the highway."

"Are you sure it's the highway?" she asked.

He mentally reviewed their walk, which had taken a zigzag course through the neighborhood. "Yeah. I'm sure. In fact, your car should be parked in the next block unless my internal compass has gone completely haywire."

"You don't see the car, Brian?"

He turned toward her, realizing that he'd revealed more of his sight loss than he had intended. She, more than anyone except Sam, seemed tuned in to him, making it impossible for him to hide.

She held her hand in front of her face and closed her thumb and forefinger together, making a circle that was no more than an inch in diameter. "That's all you can see, isn't it?" She stepped closer to him so they were separated by no more than two feet. "If I'm here you can see me." She took a couple of steps, then disappeared from his field of vision. "And now you can't."

Turning his head, he found her watching him with concern. He saw the same expression on too many faces these days, and he hated it. "I have things that have to be taken care of before this—" he waved a hand in front of his eyes "—is gone."

"You've said that before." She was silent a moment then said, "Let's go back to Guardian Paws and then you can get to those things."

Her tone was neutral enough, but he had the feeling she was annoyed.

He commanded the dog forward and they headed for her car, which was a scant block away, just as he had thought.

At the vehicle, she unlocked the doors, and held the rear one open for Jasper. Brian gave the dog the command to climb in, and as he closed the door behind the dog, realized that Angela's attention was on something else. He followed the line of her gaze, which was on another car in the parking lot of a café across the street. She glanced back at Brian, then into the backseat of her car where Jasper sat. Without a word, she got into the car. After giving the vehicle a long look, Brian did, as well, his shoulder brushing hers as he curled into the seat of her small car.

As she put the key into the ignition, he asked, "Is that Tommy over there? Is he stalking you?"

"No, that wasn't Tommy." She didn't add anything

further as she put the vehicle into gear and pulled away from the curb. After being outside, the interior of the car felt warm, comfortable, though he couldn't stretch out his legs.

"You didn't answer the other question."

"Is he stalking me?" she repeated. "He's being a pain, but it hasn't come to that. If it does, I'll handle it."

He listened to the nuance in her voice, thinking about his brag that his other senses were heightened. He wished it were so in this case. He had the feeling she was annoyed, but whether about the car she had looked at so carefully or something else, he couldn't tell.

When they stopped at a traffic light, he asked, "Did we cut today's training time short?"

"A bit," she said. "But we still covered everything that I wanted."

"Good."

"You do need more practice time." She was silent a moment then said, "All the things you need to take care of, I can understand that. But today you kept losing track of what we're doing. And I get the feeling it's because you're thinking about all the other demands on your time."

When she turned her head to look at him, he saw it only because he was watching her, the world beyond her face reduced to a black void.

"When you're working with Jasper you need to be right here," she added, "thinking about this."

"I understand." His coaches had expected the same thing during practice. No thinking about the next game or anything else off the field. Just focus on the drill you were doing right now.

Her voice softened and she launched into a debriefing of their time together, praising him for the things he'd done well, offering diplomatic suggestions for the things that were giving him trouble. He'd been right to call her "coach" because her approach was exactly the right blend of discipline and encouragement.

When they arrived at Guardian Paws, he could see that Sam had arrived and was waiting for him inside the SUV. Angela didn't immediately get out of the car, and Brian looked toward her. She met his gaze, her own eyes shadowed.

"Have you gone public with your sight loss?"

"Not yet. Those things I keep telling you about— one of them is an endorsement contract with the National Milk Association that I want to wrap up before I go public."

She looked away. "That car back there—the guy in it was a reporter who came to see me earlier in the week. He wants to do a feature on Guardian Paws."

Since the paper had recently published a feature on his foundation, Brian knew how positive that could be for the organization. "How come I hear a 'but' in that?"

"He's that investigative reporter, Andrew—"

"Brogg," Brian finished, that cold stone of worry once more dropping into his stomach. The man had been hounding him for an interview for weeks. He'd gotten a lot more persistent after one of the kids involved with the Beanstalk Gang had been picked up on a gang-related charge a couple of weeks ago. "And he's doing a feature?" That didn't quite make sense, given the man's reputation as a hard-nosed investigative reporter.

"That's what he says. He sold Maisey on a 'feel-good story.'"

Brian thought he understood what she wasn't saying—that she didn't trust Brogg. Brian didn't, either, but he had cause.

"I'm pretty sure he saw you working with Jasper," Angela said, "which is something I should have thought about before we headed to a public street. It never occurred to me that you'd be recognized."

"You couldn't have anticipated that."

Sam had warned Brian that the reporter seemed to be following them, as recently as the day they had met Angela at the chamber of commerce luncheon. Until now, Brian had dismissed that as coincidence. As reassuring as he tried to be with Angela, he had his own ideas about Andrew Brogg's agenda. Brian couldn't imagine the man writing a feel-good story, so Angela's instincts about that were dead-on. Conceited as it seemed to even contemplate it, Brian was positive the reporter's interest in Guardian Paws was solely related to his connection to them.

Angela didn't deserve any negative fallout as a result of his problems any more than National Milk Association did. Turning the possibilities over in his mind, Brian decided he needed to contact them today even though plans to shoot the next commercial were already under way.

Bottom line, his ability to release the story of his

sight loss the way he wanted was fast spinning out of control.

Out of control.

The three words he hated most.

Angela arrived at the Larimer Grill at the appointed time that same evening with one thing on her mind—finding out what Andrew Brogg hoped to accomplish by following her. If he wanted the "feel-good" feature he was trying to convince her of, he needed to change his tactics.

The restaurant was filled with people who were squeezed together around tables that were too close together. The noise level was loud. The place was, she decided, an odd choice for an interview—they'd have to shout at one another to be heard. Within the bar area, a loud cheer went up in response to the football game flickering across several big-screen televisions.

Finally she spotted Andrew toward the back of the restaurant, seated in a booth where he had a clear view of one of the televisions.

"You have a strange idea of where to conduct an interview," Angela said as she sat down.

"Nice to see you, too," he said without any heat, signaling a waiter. "What will you have to drink?"

"Water," Angela told the waiter, "with lemon." She put her purse in her lap and leaned toward Andrew. "What were you doing in Brighton this afternoon? Or maybe I should ask, why you were watching me?"

"And good evening to you, too. You're looking pretty tonight," he said.

She gave the man a sharp look. "I repeat. Why were you watching me this afternoon?"

"I wanted to see you working."

"Oh, please."

"It's the truth."

"If it is, what's the rest of it?"

He shrugged and picked up his glass. "You tell me."

The waiter returned with her water and inquired if they were ready to order.

"I'll have a burger," Angela said, not bothering with the menu.

Andrew told the waiter that he'd have the same, then said, "You have your ways of doing things, and I have mine."

"Mine don't include sneaking around and watching like some spy."

"And what about before you went to prison?" he returned.

At last it was in the open, she thought. "My prison record isn't a secret."

Once more, he shrugged. "You don't talk about it much, either. Like, for instance, at the luncheon you spoke at the other day."

She drew a blank for a second before remembering the chamber of commerce luncheon.

"I was there to talk about Guardian Paws, not my past."

He leaned toward her, his smile back and his eyes unreadable behind the lens of his glasses. "So it's a 'bad girl turns her life around and makes good'. That's what you're telling me, right?"

She watched him, wishing she knew what he was thinking.

He sighed. "Okay, I admit it. Old habits die hard. For the kind of stories I usually do, you find out more by observing when people don't know you're watching. And then, when you do get to talk to them, it's an adversarial process sometimes. I didn't mean for us to get off on the wrong foot."

"If you want to know something about me, ask. That's the way we'll do this."

"Why was Brian Ramsey with you this afternoon?"

She realized belatedly she had backed herself into a corner. The interview—or whatever it was—had gone from bad to much worse.

"If that wasn't Brian Ramsey," Andrew said, "it was someone who could be his double."

"Let's talk about Guardian Paws," she said. "Or the dogs."

"Is he a friend or a donor or a client—"

"Or the training methods we use," she tacked on.

"So you don't want to answer the question."

"He's a friend," she said. That was true, so far as it went. She did consider Brian a friend. "As for clients, I don't want to talk about anyone by name unless I have their permission."

"Fair enough," Andrew agreed. "How did you meet Ramsey?"

"We can talk about Guardian Paws or I'm leaving," she said.

Andrew shrugged. "You can't blame me for asking." He gave her a self-deprecating smile. "I'm a lowly reporter and you're dating a rich jock. A guy does what he can to compete. You know?"

"You're not that lowly," Angela said. "And I am not dating Brian."

"You're 'just friends,'" Andrew said, gesturing quote marks in the air. "Okay, then. Tell me about this training you're so keen on."

Someone came to a stop next to the booth, and Angela looked up expecting to see the waiter. Instead, Tommy met her gaze, his Cheshire-cat grin on his face.

"Here you are," he said, sliding into the booth and pushing her farther into the space. Extending his hand to Andrew, whose expression of surprise matched how Angela felt, Tommy added, "Tommy Manderoll."

"What are you doing here?" she asked, wanting to push him out of the booth, wanting to shout at him for once more intruding into her life.

He waved the hand that Andrew hadn't shaken. "I saw you come in, and just had to stop in and say hello. Aren't you going to introduce your friend?"

"Andrew Brogg, reporter for the *Denver Chronicle*," the journalist said. "I'm doing a feature on Guardian Paws."

"You don't say? A reporter." Tommy folded his hand around Angela's. "Wonderful things my girl is doing there. About time someone noticed."

Angela pulled her hand free. "I am not your girl, and this is a business meeting—"

"And you want me to leave," Tommy filled in. He shook his head, managing to somehow look contrite. "I guess I did barge in." His voice trailed off as though he expected her to disagree with him. Ending the awkward silence that followed, he leaned over and kissed her cheek. "Well. I've got to be going. Call me."

The waiter arrived with their meals as Tommy slid out of the booth. Embarrassed and angry and needing to collect her thoughts, Angela stared at the table while the waiter made small talk and set down their plates.

After he was gone, she raised her head and looked at Andrew. "I'm not dating him, either."

"Gotcha," he said.

Only Angela knew that Andrew could easily find out they had once dated and that Tommy had testified against her. It didn't take any great leap of imagination to put the worst possible spin on his intrusion.

So much for providing Andrew with the right tone for the "feel-good" story. Deciding there was no point to continuing the charade, she set down her fork and picked up her purse. "I've got to go."

Surprise, then irritation, flickered across his face. "Don't do something you're going to regret."

But the warning was too late—she already had.

SIX

"Well, that is some story," said Kenneth Upton, the chairman of the National Milk Association. He and the association attorney sat across the conference room table from Brian, his attorney and his manager.

Brian had just finished reading the statement the three of them had crafted last night after Angela had spotted Andrew Brogg. The statement fell considerably short of what Brian had wanted to say, but covered the basics of his sight loss and the reasons for it, including his abuse of anabolic steroids early in his career. He steadily met Upton's gaze, remembering how pleased he had been when they had offered him a position as spokesman four years earlier. His poster was featured prominently on the conference room wall with other celebrities far more famous than him.

"That's all Mr. Upton has to say at this time," said the association attorney. Brian turned his head slightly so he could see her. Her hair was styled in a smooth, severe cut and she was dressed in a black suit and red blouse that Brian knew was supposed to make her look powerful and invincible. A comparison to Angela's soft eyes and the curling wisps of hair around her face feathered through his mind, a look he far preferred over this woman's sophistication.

"We expected no more," said Brian's attorney, Gil York.

Personally, Brian would have preferred both of the attorneys and his manager to have taken a hike so he and Kenneth could have a conversation without everyone worried about protecting their respective positions. Had his sight been intact, a discussion over the fourth tee at Castle Pines Golf Club would have been about right.

Kenneth smiled slightly as though he'd had a similar thought, his expression far different than the stoic one of his attorney.

"How much sight do you have left?" he asked, his tone absent of the soft pseudo-sympathy that drove Brian nuts.

"Very little," he replied. "I gave up driving a while ago."

"But you don't use a white cane yet," the attorney said.

Brian turned his head so he could see her. "No. That would be going public with my sight loss, and I wasn't ready for that."

"And just how do we know all this is true?" she asked.

Brian nodded toward Gil. "Give her the copies of the medical records."

Gil set his briefcase on the table and snapped it open, taking out a sheaf of papers. Pulling a pen from the inside pocket of his suit, he handed both to her. "Please sign the top sheet that you've received these and that this information is to be kept in confidence until after Brian has issued a press release."

She read the cover sheet, drew a line through one phrase and initialed it, and said, "We're not going to agree to wait a month." She signed at the bottom. "If what you say is true, this secret is already out of the bag."

"Yes, it probably is," said Brian's manager, Dwight Davidson. "We believe it's in everyone's best interests to wait—"

"For you to put a 'positive spin' on this?" the association attorney interrupted.

"You have my word we won't leak this," Kenneth said, standing. "But we all know how the media gets when it smells a story. So, my strong advice is for you to get your ducks lined up."

"We're doing our best." Brian stood and offered the association president his hand. "I wanted you to hear this from me before it hits the papers."

"I appreciate that." He shook Brian's hand.

"I want you to know...being your spokesman is something I've been proud of."

The association attorney came around the end of the table. "You do realize this may alter our commitment—"

"We understand that," Dwight interrupted the other attorney. "But we still expect to shoot the commercial next week as planned."

"Might as well, since it's already scheduled," Kenneth said, tone mild. He nodded toward Brian. "And we'll be in touch."

"I'll make a copy of this and be right back," the association attorney said, waving the cover sheet.

"Good luck to you," Kenneth said, following her down the hall.

Gil and Dwight made small talk while they waited for the attorney to return with the cover sheet. The instant they were out of the office and into the elevator, their demeanor changed.

"I told you this was a mistake," Gil said as the elevator doors closed and the car began its descent.

"I thought it went pretty well," Dwight said.

"Are you crazy?" Gil exclaimed. "Their counsel is going to be poring over the contract looking for the breach that we just provided. We're going to be left holding the bag."

"It was the right thing," Brian said. "We all know what's going to happen over the next couple of weeks if Andrew Brogg jumps to conclusions. It's going to be a circus. And I want the fallout to be right here." He tapped the middle of his chest. "If they want to go public with this first, I don't care."

"It could hurt your foundation," Dwight said. "You've already got problems there thanks to the arrest of that kid—"

"That 'kid' has a name. Ivan Fletcher."

"Dwight is right," Gil added. "That 'kid's' arrest is trouble, no matter how innocent he wants to make you think he is."

"I think he's telling the truth," Brian said. He had

personally talked with Ivan, shooting hoops with the kid in an effort to get him to relax and open up. He denied the accusation that he'd sold drugs to an undercover cop. His older brother and two other young men had been arrested along with Ivan, so Brian figured the cops had decided he was guilty by association.

"That's because he reminds you of yourself, by your own admission," Dwight said as the elevator came to a stop.

"You can't compete with the lure of gang life and easy money," Gil added.

"Don't be telling me I'm on a fool's mission," Brian said, stepping out of the elevator and facing the two men. He'd been listening to variations of the same warning since he'd first started the program. One of its risks came with working with kids from low-income families and a rough-around-the-edges life. "I don't want to hear it." He looked around the big lobby of the building, a bank on one side and a Starbucks on the other. "Do you see Sam?"

"Right there in front of the Starbucks," Gil said.

Brian turned his head twice before spotting him, the black void larger than his field of vision. He looked back at Dwight and Gil, knowing both men were doing their jobs in trying to protect him with their dire warnings about coming clean with the NMA and about Ivan Fletcher. "Thanks for coming with me today." He tapped Gil on the shoulder. "And stop worrying."

"You pay me to worry." He waved, moving away. "Talk to you in a couple of days."

"Two words for you," Dwight said.

"Only two?"

The manager grinned. "I'm running late, so yeah, only two. Get the mess with Ivan straightened out." He took a breath. "And don't underestimate Andrew Brogg. He's mean to the bone, and he's got a particular grudge against celebrity athletes."

Doing her best to clear her mind of the disastrous meeting with Andrew Brogg, Angela drove up the winding driveway of Brian's home, which was in a gated community southwest of downtown. Far better to think of Rachel, who had surprised her last night by inviting her to Thanksgiving dinner. Though she and Rachel had once catered to wealthy clients in Aspen, it had been a long time since she had been in so grand a neighborhood.

"Would you look at that?" she murmured when the house came into view. French-inspired architecture took advantage of the view of Mount Evans, which rose west of Denver. In the morning light it was brilliant with a recent snowfall, and it took no leap of imagination to visualize this home in the Alps instead of a few miles outside of Denver. She parked the car and got out, taking in every detail that she could. She had imagined Brian living in a house that had modern, clean lines rather than this one that inspired visions of a French château. Opening the door for Jasper, she looked back the way she had come. The yard was inviting and surprisingly cozy given its scale.

What drew her attention, though, was a Nativity scene that looked so lifelike Angela first thought she was looking at real people. The tableau had been set up so it faced the house. She turned her head toward it, wondering if the window that overlooked this area was the breakfast room. And she admitted it surprised her since Brian hadn't struck her as a religious man.

The house itself was decked out in Christmas splendor, including pungent cut evergreens artfully arranged in a window box and a simple wreath on the front door, which was recessed inside a circular entryway. The place was one of the most beautiful homes she had ever seen.

Her smile faded as she thought of the man it belonged to—a man who wouldn't be able to see its splendor much longer.

She rang the bell and heard the chimes ringing inside.

Next to her, Jasper cocked his head as though listening to sounds from inside that she couldn't hear. After a long minute, she rang the bell once more.

When no one came to the door after another minute, Angela tried the door, which, to her surprise, opened.

"Hello," she called, stepping into the foyer. "Is anyone home?"

No sound but the echo of her own voice. The foyer was huge and so perfectly put together it could have been featured in *Architectural Digest*. As she called again, she fleetingly wondered if anyone played the grand piano tucked beneath the arching staircase or if it was purely ornamental.

Next to her Jasper whined softly, his attention fixed on a hallway off to the left.

"Brian?"

"I'm in the kitchen."

She followed the sound of his voice, going through a butler's pantry next to a dining room that would comfortably seat twenty and into the kitchen. It and the adjoining, sunlit and inviting breakfast area, were easily as big as her whole house. She didn't see Brian.

"Where are you?"

His head came up from behind a large island in the middle of the room, his expression filled with frustration.

"Hi," she said, coming around the corner. Broken china was scattered across the ceramic tile floor. He was on his hands and knees, sweeping up the shards. A plant was lying on its side, the pot broken and soil spilling onto the floor. Of more concern was blood smeared over the floor.

"Stay," she said to Jasper, making sure he was well away from the shards spread across the floor. She knelt next to Brian, picking up pieces of the china and dropping them in the wastebasket. "You look like you could use some moral support."

He gave a quick bark of laughter. "That's an understatement."

"Are you hurt?"

He shook his head even as she saw blood dripping from a cut on his hand.

"You're bleeding."

He brought his hand in front of his face, a sure sign to her that his sight was nearly gone. He stood and moved toward the sink, his mouth tight with irritation, blood dripping along the way and shards crunching under his feet. At least he wasn't barefoot.

He yanked open a drawer, and, seeing that wash-cloths were neatly stacked inside, Angela reached for one, then his hand. "You need some pressure on this, but first let's make sure the wound is clean."

"I can do it," he snapped.

This wasn't the first time she'd had a client be upset with a situation surrounding the loss of control that came with a disability. This was, though, the first time the irritation felt personal.

"Fine." She took a step away from him. "Where do you keep the broom?"

"My mess, my problem," he said.

"True, but yelling at me and pushing me away doesn't help." She wanted to soothe the tension radiating from him but had the feeling he was spoiling for a fight. "Take your pick. Let me help you bandage up your hand or sweep the floor."

He turned toward her, and her sympathy for him grew as she watched him search for her before his gaze lit on her. "Since I'm unlikely to bleed to death..." He sighed as though what he was about to say didn't please him. "The broom is in a closet in the laundry room." He waved at a door on the far side of the room.

"Stay," she said to Jasper as she headed for the closed door.

Brian watched her go before turning his attention back to the cut on the side of his hand. He probed at it, satisfying himself that nothing was in the cut. Applying pressure to the cut, he turned around and looked at the mess he had created. What he could see of it was revealed to him in small bits as he slowly turned his head, his vision gone except for a tiny hole that was like looking through a hole about the size of a nickel.

His remaining vision was a fraction of what it had been when he'd gone to bed last night. He hated that his sight was nearly gone, and his chest had felt like he was buried beneath a couple of NFL tackles all day. He hadn't told his grandparents about the sudden reduction in his vision, but he'd put in a call to the ophthalmologist shortly after they had left for their weekly lunch date with a retired crony of Gramps's. The ophthalmologist had reminded him they had talked about how his sight could stabilize or be gone within a few days.

Brian knew now that it would be gone soon. The out-of-control feeling that had been spiraling like a wild Slinky toy tumbling down the stairs made his palms sweat and his heart pound. And it didn't go away no matter how much he pretended he was fine. He wasn't prepared for this.

He heard Angela returning to the kitchen and lifted his head to find her. She looked in his direction, and though he couldn't see the broom, he heard the swish of it on the floor.

"What happened?" she asked a moment later.

"I was getting the Christmas dishes out of the top shelf of the cabinet and I slipped," he said, wishing he had ignored Nonnie's request to get them down. "My grandmother is going to kill me."

"These were hers?" Angela asked.

"Were?" He shook his head. "They still are. My

grandparents live here with me. These dishes have been her pride and joy every year for as long as I can remember. Each Christmas she'd buy another place setting." Vividly, he remembered the year he'd saved enough of his allowance to purchase her a set of salt and pepper shakers, and he wondered if they had been among the casualties when he had lost his balance and dropped the dinner plates.

He couldn't hear the broom, so he turned his head until he found Angela, who wasn't sweeping, but instead was watching him.

"What?" he asked.

"Do your parents live here, too?" she asked.

"No."

She started sweeping again. "I think this pattern is open stock."

"You think?"

"I can make the call for you, if you want."

Some of the pressure in his chest eased. "I'd appreciate that." He hadn't gotten that far in his thinking. The china was expensive enough that it had been collected over many years. Ironically, he could afford to buy Nonnie whatever she wanted...and though he intended to do that, he knew it wouldn't be the same since she knew the origin of every chip and scratch.

"How long have your grandparents lived here?"

He heard the tinkling sound that indicated she had swept the china into the dustpan and dumped it in the wastebasket.

"Since I bought the house. They raised me," he said.

"My mother died when I was seven," she said.

He lifted his head to look at her, unable to see anything of her expression since her head was bent.

A moment later she raised it, her face pink, her gaze seeking his. "I didn't mean to tell you that. You know—make it sound like my childhood was worse than yours. I just meant that I know what that might have felt like."

"Mine abandoned me. She didn't get around to dying until I was in college." He had no idea why he was telling her this. He didn't talk about his mother. "If that sounds bitter, well, that's just the way it is."

"I remember feeling that way." She picked up several shards of china that were under the kick plate next to the sink. "Do you want the stuff in the wastebasket taken to the garbage can?"

"I can do it," he said.

She stared at him without saying a word, and he stared back at her through the small hole of his vision. Sighing, he gave in. "It's in the back of the garage."

She smiled. "That wasn't so bad, now, was it?" She headed once more toward the hallway. "Take a load off and talk to Jasper."

Brian had forgotten about the dog, which embarrassed him. He found the dog lying on the floor next to the table. He crossed the room and pulled out a chair. "You've been a patient boy," he told the dog, who rose to a sitting position when Brian sat down. He hadn't given a bit of thought to the potential dangers all this glass represented. That fast, the constriction in his chest was back. He hadn't considered the responsibility of making sure the dog was safe, or the hazards a simple thing like broken glass could present to the animal.

Mostly though, his mind remained on Angela's confession about her mother's death. He stood, his attention fixed on the hallway, waiting for the moment when she would appear out of the dark void and into his line of vision.

At once, there she was, her light brown hair mussed in comparison to the sleek sophistication of the National Milk Association attorney. Angela smiled when she realized he was watching her, and he absorbed everything about the expression. He could spend a lifetime studying the nuance of her expressions. Except he didn't have a lifetime. He might have only today.

"When did you stop being bitter?" he asked, knowing his tone sounded too demanding but needing to know.

"When I stopped living in the past."

Her answer was immediate, automatic.

"That simple?"

She chuckled, and he realized she often did at his direct questions instead of taking offense as most people he knew would have. "Simple? Yes. But not easy. The simple things rarely are."

"How did she die?" He knew the question sounded too blunt, too intrusive, but he wanted to know what made her tick, where her seemingly deep reservoir of calm came from.

"Leukemia." Angela raised her head and looked outside.

Brian followed her line of vision and saw that she was looking at the Nativity scene in the side yard.

"The funny thing is," she continued, "that I didn't

know until after I was an adult and read her death certificate. I don't remember her being sick until about two or three weeks before she died. One day she was there, and the next she was in the hospital, and right after that she was gone." She smiled, but it wasn't a happy expression, but one turned inward. "And since Dad stopped eating dinner with me after that, I was sure her dying was my fault and that was why he never came home."

Her lips tightened as though she had revealed more than she intended. Brian watched her as she sat down, relating to what she'd said since his mother hadn't loved him enough to stick around.

"And so, the obvious answer to that was to be in control." She lifted her head then and looked at him. "Make sure no one can ever make me that vulnerable again."

Her eyes were bright with emotion, and his own felt gritty with it. She could have been talking about him.

SEVEN

"Why are you asking me about this, Brian?"

He wasn't at all sure how to put his thoughts into words. "Nothing much ever seems to ruffle you."

She laughed.

"A part of me wanted to believe that was because you don't have any problems. Stupid, I know that. Everyone has problems, but you know what I mean."

"That it would be easy to be happy if you had no problems or challenges?" She shook her head. "We both know that's a fairy tale."

"Happy is one thing. But you're calm. I'd give anything to feel a tenth of that."

She smiled. "Beware of what you ask for."

"Because?"

"Most people don't want to talk about God or religion or faith. My calm, as you put it, comes from knowing that I'm doing God's will and knowing that He has a plan for me that's filled only with good."

"Turn things over to God?" Brian shook his head. "I don't think so. He's got His hands full."

When he looked at her, he saw that she was gazing

outside toward the Nativity scene again. Her expression was wistful.

"That came out harsher than I intended," he said. "Sorry about that. If you're into all that religious stuff and—"

"I am." She turned her head and looked at him.

"I didn't mean to step on your toes."

"You didn't." Angela's soft smile was back. "Once I was just as skeptical as you are and just as ready to run anytime anyone got close to the *G* word even though my best friend's dad is a minister."

The *G* word? The reference made him smile since the summation was on target. He'd brought this conversation on himself.

"But you're not anymore?" He didn't know why he was asking, but he kept having this idea that she had answers he wanted.

"Skeptical? No."

He reached across the table for her hand. "How is it that we both have mothers who died and you got religion and I didn't? All my life, I felt like I could disappear, and it wouldn't really matter. At least you had faith."

She shook her head. "But I didn't. Not until a couple of years ago."

Her fingers felt cool next to his, and he prayed she wouldn't take her hand away. Prayed. A figure of speech or something more? He wished he knew.

She watched him as though weighing what to say to him. "All those problems you just mentioned? God doesn't swoop down from heaven in some grand gesture. He works for us by working through us. That's the point of the Golden Rule."

"That whole do unto others business—"

"Exactly. Remember what you said to me the first day we met?" She took a breath. "That meeting me was an answer to a prayer."

That had been exactly his thought that day. He'd arrived at the luncheon discouraged because his sight was decreasing at such a rapid rate and because the last of his applications for a guide dog had been returned, putting him at the back of a long waiting list. Then Angela had stood up for her demonstration with Polly, and since he had almost not attended that day, he'd felt as though he was supposed to have been there. A literal answer to a prayer, though? No way.

"That's an expression."

"Easy to dismiss, too," she agreed. "Since many prayers appear to go unanswered."

He grinned. "I have the feeling that agreeing with you is going to come back and bite me."

She smiled back. "But of course."

She still hadn't pulled her hand away, which surprised him. He liked this connection with her and couldn't have said when he last held hands with anyone—not even Erica before they had broken up.

"Are you ready to get to work?" she asked.

Her evident perception that he was ready to let go of the conversation surprised him. "What? You're not going to invite me to church?"

"Is that what you want?" she countered.

"Not yet," he said after a moment's pause while he

wondered what she prayed for. If her prayers were indeed answered, she clearly didn't pray for material things. The home she lived in was quite a lot smaller and far more modest than the one he'd lived in with Nonnie and Gramps when he was a boy. Angela's car had been old five years ago. And she also had none of the usual awe for his lifestyle that many had. He'd give a huge amount to have one ounce of her tranquility even though he wasn't ready to go to church. "Maybe someday."

She handed him Jasper's leash and harness. "Let's get to work, then."

His glance fell to Jasper, who patiently lay at their feet. "Okay, but I have a favor to ask." When she raised her eyebrows, he said, "When we're finished will you take me shopping so I can replace my grandmother's dishes?"

"Okay," she said, her ready agreement surprising him. Surely she had dozens of things to do besides hang out with him.

"And one more thing?" He smiled at her, hoping she'd understand. "Can we please take my car?"

She laughed. "Tired of sitting with your knees next to your chin, huh?"

"Yep." Her ability to see the humor of him in her small car drew him. Looking at her right now, he knew his vow to keep the relationship on a purely professional level was crumbling by the second. "I know I'm imposing."

"Oh, yeah. Life is hard," she teased. "I have to go shopping for really nice china and drive an Escalade."

The cell phone in Brian's pocket rang. Setting down the leash, he reached for it, recognizing the ringtone he'd assigned to the administrative assistant for the Beanstalk Gang, Jodie Clark, since he could no longer read the caller ID.

"Hey, Jodie," he said.

Affable as the greeting was, Angela realized something was terribly wrong an instant later as his demeanor went from relaxed to completely focused, his tone of voice terse.

"You're there now?… You're sure the building is empty? Maybe you should wait in the car until the police arrive. I'll be there within the hour." He disconnected the call.

"What's happened?" she asked.

"Someone has broken into our offices," he said. "And I just remembered that I didn't expect to need Sam this week, so he's gone to Vail to ski. He won't be back until after Thanksgiving" He raked a hand through his hair, his frustration evident in every gesture. "And my grandparents are at a lunch. They're not due back until late afternoon. I've got to call a taxi and then—"

"Stop." Angela took his hands and made sure she was standing within his line of vision. "I'll drive you."

His reaction to her statement was an expression of complete astonishment. "You'd do that? I have no idea how long this will take—"

"It takes as long as it takes," she said, letting go of his hands. "Possibly not as much fun as shopping—"

"I can't let you."

"Why not?" She set her hands on her hips. "You can call your taxi, or we can get in the car and go."

"This is exactly the thing I've feared most about losing my sight," he said, his frown back. "Being dependent upon others. I hate it. I really hate it."

She resisted the urge to smooth out the deep furrows between his eyebrows. "I can understand that."

"We're taking my car," he said, heading toward the back hallway.

"I figured we would," she said, picking up her coat and Jasper's leash, which she snapped onto his collar. She followed him past the laundry room where Brian waited, holding the door to the garage open for her.

"Thanks," he said as she came past him, holding out the keys for her. "I owe you."

"Stop it," she softly said, this time giving in to the urge to touch him, giving his chest a reassuring pat. "This is what friends do for each other."

And she knew she had crossed a threshold with this man, one that she had vowed she wouldn't. That headline that haunted her flashed through her mind—The Felon and the Football Player. He was more in need of a friend than he knew, and though she had just signed herself up for the job, she needed to make sure she stayed in the shadows of his life. For both their sakes.

That proved impossible, though, because when they arrived at the Beanstalk Gang office on Colorado Boulevard, Brian took her hand when they got out of the car. He didn't let go as they made their way past a television news crew and several police vehicles. How could she have forgotten they'd be here? Angela wondered as they made their way around vehicles and came to a stop at the crime-scene tape marking a perimeter.

Brian identified himself, and the officer lifted the tape, motioning for them to come through. A gaping hole was where a plate glass window should have been. Within a few steps, Angela realized that Brian was letting her lead him around the obstacles. She looked at him, wondering how much of his sight was left, as they walked through the broken glass that crunched underfoot. They stepped inside the building where a pretty African-American woman was talking to two men. She excused herself the minute she saw Brian and came toward them.

"I am so glad you're here," she said, coming toward him, her eyes wide and worried.

"Jodie Clark, this is Angela London."

"Ah, the dog trainer. Nice to meet you." She took Brian by the arm and stepped close, whispering, "The detectives think this was an inside job."

Angela wasn't sure she'd ever seen a bigger mess. Anything that could be turned over or smashed had been, down to a water dispenser that was leaking all over the carpet. A breeze swept in from outside, making the room cold.

"When I got here, the alarm was already off." Jodie waved a hand around the room. "Whoever was in here had a lot of time."

Brian squeezed her hand. "We'll get to the bottom of it."

"I know. But …" She glanced at Angela then lowered

her voice once more, "They are asking a lot of questions about Ivan."

"Besides the damage, any idea on what is missing?" Brian asked.

"I've been working on a list." Jodie headed back toward a reception desk that sat behind a half wall.

"How many obstacles are between me and the detectives over there?" Brian softly asked Angela, once more taking her hand.

"An overturned chair halfway between," she said, "and a bunch of papers strewn across the floor."

He let go of her hand, and she stepped in front of him, picking up the chair and carrying it toward Jodie's desk while Brian introduced himself to the two detectives.

"Is there anything I can do to help?" she asked Jodie.

Jodie looked up from her list and shook her head. "At the moment I don't even know where to start."

Angela looked back at the front of the building where a jagged shard of glass jutted up from the bottom sill. Another officer joined the one they had met outside, and beyond them, the news crew stood on the outside of the crime-scene tape that had been put up since they came in.

"Do you have a regular handyman we can call to board up the windows?" she asked.

"I—" Jodie looked around, her expression growing more distressed. "I don't even know," she finished, picking up a sheet of paper and taking it to Brian.

Angela watched him thank Jodie, but he didn't look at the paper. His attention was on the detective, his head cocked in the way she recognized when he was really concentrating, his expression grim and his free hand shoved into his pocket.

"Too many things aren't adding up," the detective was saying to Brian. "We had Miss Clark—" he pointed at Jodie "—test the alarm system, and it appears to be in working order though it never went off during this incident." He waved toward a whiteboard behind the reception desk that had obscenities written on it. "This looks like the work of someone holding a grudge, someone who knows his way around your facility. Do you have any disgruntled employees?"

"No," Brian said.

One of the officers headed toward Angela. "I saw you come in with Mr. Ramsey," he said. "Who are you?"

"Angela London," she replied evenly, reminding herself she had no reason to be nervous around this man. Unlike when she had single-handedly destroyed the business she had been in with her best friend, Rachel. Nothing about this place or this day should so vividly remind her of the day she had been arrested, but she was uncomfortable nonetheless.

"And your relationship with him is?"

Angela looked past the man at Brian, remembering what she'd told him earlier. "A friend." The truth, just not the exact truth.

"Your name is really familiar," he said, studying her face. "Probably from the society pages."

She shrugged without answering. His conclusion made sense, she decided, that any friend of Brian's would be the sort the detective had alluded to. Thankfully, most people didn't remember the news from four years ago when her name had been plastered all over the local media, but police officers weren't "most people." She was no longer naive, and she knew the detective would be back with questions when he made the connection.

"You know anyone who might have a grudge against Mr. Ramsey or the work this Beanstalk Gang does?"

Angela shook her head.

He handed her a business card. "If you think of anyone, you'll call?"

Doing her best to ignore her memories of the last time a detective had questioned her, Angela looked down at the card and read his name—Sergeant John Venters, Detective. "Sure thing, Detective Venters."

He moved away, and she gave an inward sigh. What had she been thinking when she had offered to drive Brian here? At some level, she had to have known there would be lots of police and even more questions of anyone in the vicinity. She was a law-abiding person who just happened to be a felon. And she knew that in her case, any knowledge of her background could only make things worse for Brian. In that moment, she wanted to find the back way out and slink away.

Bits of her conversation with Brian flitted through her head. Funny that he thought she was so calm, a perception that would be shattered if he could see the turmoil inside of her.

EIGHT

A thousand and one details vied for Brian's attention as the police came and went. Calls to the insurance adjuster. Finding someone to board up the windows. He also called the house and left a message for his grandparents since he'd taken off in too big a hurry to let them know his plans had changed and he wouldn't be home for the day.

Each time felt as though he were being swallowed by the chaos, he'd catch Angela's gaze. Her calm presence soothed him, and from the looks of things she had the same effect on Jodie, who was a lot more settled down than she had been a couple of hours ago.

Eventually, the police all left, and Brian went outside to talk to the two camera crews that had been waiting all afternoon. The day was shot, and right now he couldn't remember what his plans had been before Jodie's call.

Taking his time to focus on each reporter's face, Brian told them the break-in appeared to be a simple case of vandalism. Evidently satisfied no exciting scoop was to be had, the two crews moved away. Behind them stood Andrew Brogg.

"I heard the police talking about Ivan Fletcher," he said. "Is he a suspect?"

"You'll have to ask the detectives in charge of the case," Brian returned.

"Isn't it true that you're protecting him, that you were instrumental in getting the drug charges against him dropped?"

These were the kinds of questions that Brian hated, the ones that started with part of a fact and ended with a whole lot of innuendo—the kind of question to which there was no acceptable answer. An outright denial wasn't the truth, but an admission wasn't, either. Since Brogg seemed to have his own agenda, no matter what Brian said, he knew it was likely any answer would be taken out of context.

"You were at the hearing," Brian finally said. "The court record speaks for itself."

"That's double talk," Brogg said, stepping closer. His voice dropped. "Come clean about your activities with Val Fitzwater, and I'll make the rest of the story look good."

"And here I thought the truth is what you were after," Brian said, staring at the man. "As for my old teammate, I haven't heard from him or spoken to him in years."

"Maybe because he's serving a prison term for pushing drugs."

"You seem to have all the pertinent facts."

"And you still claim you were never were involved in selling steroids."

"Never was," Brian said. "I thought you were gathering information on today's crime, not rehashing old news."

"With drugs and kids, there's no such thing as old news. I know your kind, and sooner or later I'll have you."

His tone was vehement, as though Brian himself had somehow caused the man trouble. "Did I ever do anything to you?" he asked.

Andrew made a show of putting his notebook away and turning off his tape recorder. "Besides manipulating the law to suit your own twisted purposes or setting up the perfect front to peddle steroids and other illegal drugs to kids? Nah." He gave a mock salute. "Happy Thanksgiving."

Shocked at the hatred dripping from the man's voice, Brian watched him cross the street and get into his car. So there it was, if he took Brogg's statement at face value. The man believed he was peddling drugs, saw him as a danger to the kids he wanted to help. And, given the man's reputation for drawing blood with his articles, Brian knew he had a major PR battle on his hands. If only he knew where to start.

He turned around and looked at the boarded-up windows and well-lit parking lot. At the moment, the place looked too much like one of the graffiti-covered, abandoned storefronts that had once dotted the neighborhood.

He headed back inside where the coaches and other staff had come in from all over the city to pitch in to get things cleaned up. Angela was in the middle of the activity, talking and helping out as though she'd always been a member of the team. After all the glass had been cleaned up, she had brought in Jasper for introductions, who greeted everyone as though they were old friends.

When he spotted Brian, he bounded across the room toward him and immediately sat in front of him, his tongue hanging out.

The dog's loyalty gave Brian an unexpected lump in his throat.

"He's just gorgeous," Jodie said, following the dog across the room. "The guys have all been telling him to sit and roll over and shake hands—playing with him like that's okay, right? I mean, Angela said it didn't hurt anything, but she did remind us that he's your dog."

"It's fine. She tells me that as long as he's in play mode, it's fine." Surprised that Angela had left that judgment to him, he searched for her. She was talking to Hank Norris, one of the coaches.

A bigger surprise was the territorial feeling that settled into the pit of Brian's stomach. He had no business wanting to stake a claim to Angela like some cave man. Still...

"And the training is going well?" Jodie asked, reclaiming Brian's attention. "He's so smart that I bet it is."

"It is," Brian said. "Jasper wasn't exactly what I was expecting, but he's great."

"I like Angela, too," Jodie added.

"Me, too." Unerringly, he found her once more, a smile lighting her face as she listened to whatever Hank was saying to her. He ought to be happy with the rapport she had developed with the staff, he told himself, instead of wishing she were laughing and smiling with him instead of Hank.

If he was truthful with himself, his feelings for her went quite a bit beyond "like." He thought about her all the time despite this being a terrible time to get involved with anyone. It was too soon after his breakup with Erica, for one thing. Plus, common sense dictated that he probably wasn't in the right place emotionally since he was in turmoil about his sight loss. But none of that reasoning made the territorial feeling go away.

Movement behind Angela snagged his attention. Dwight Davidson, his manager, came through the door, pausing to talk to a couple of people before heading in Brian's direction.

"Tell me this isn't as bad as it looks," Dwight said, striding toward him.

"The bright side is that no one was hurt," Brian said.

"All the more reason to have your offices in a secured office building instead of down here on the street in a neighborhood that is marginal at best."

"You know what I think about that," Brian returned. "Don't start." They had been having variations of this particular conversation for the last two years. Brian hadn't wanted the money they raised to go into a high-rent facility. The point was to put as much money as possible into the programs. Plus, he'd liked the idea of the offices being accessible. He had grown up in this neighborhood, so he felt that he'd returned to his roots.

Jodie moved away, and Dwight perched on the desk next to Brian. "You shouldn't be here," he said.

"Where else would I be?" Brian countered.

"Do you honestly think other celebrities are this hands-on with the work their foundations do?"

"Many of them, yes."

"Except none of them are going blind," he bluntly said. "You've got to delegate more. Let Jodie handle things. She's certainly capable enough." He took a breath. "This is the dog?"

"It is," Brian said, swallowing his annoyance at Dwight's tone.

"You can't be seen with him until after you're finished shooting the last commercial—"

"That's tomorrow," Brian said.

"Who's the pretty brunette talking to Jodie?" Dwight asked.

"Angela London." Brian homed in on her voice, thinking that Dwight had at least two things right. Jodie was capable. And Angela *was* pretty.

"The dog trainer? Why on earth did you bring her here?"

"She drove me," Brian replied, failing to keep his annoyance at Dwight's judgments out of his voice. "Let's go back to my office." He stood and led the way down the hall, away from the activity in the front room and the surprising cheer everyone had despite the problems. He closed the door after Dwight came through it. "This accusatory tone of yours has got to stop. You don't like the location of the offices. Well, nothing new there. You don't like that I came here, but this *is* my organization— ultimately I'm responsible. You imply that because I'm losing my sight, I'm suddenly incapable. Wrong. Don't treat me like I'm disabled—"

"You are disabled," Dwight said.

"No. I'm not." Brian swallowed the awful panic and even worse anger that engulfed him every time that word was mentioned. "And I won't have you treating me as though I am. Especially not in front of my staff."

"I'm looking out for you. Same as always."

"Same as always, there's one quarterback to a team. Your criticism of me stops right here."

"Point taken," Dwight conceded. Smiling, he lifted his fist.

Brian tapped it with his own. Another realization surfaced—now that he was no longer a professional athlete, this was a relationship that needed to change. "See you in the morning at the photo shoot?" he asked.

"I'll be there. Need a lift?"

"Nope. Gramps said he'd drive, and he gets a kick out of hanging around the crew, so I like having him there."

After Dwight left, Brian stared around his impossibly dark office a moment, wishing he could see better. *Disabled.* That one single word made him shake inside. Ruthlessly, he pushed the fear from his mind, squared his shoulders and went back to the front office.

Jasper came trotting toward him as he had before. Somehow, that dissolved the last of Brian's irritation as he patted the dog. His confidence bolstered, he looked around at the staff, many of these people ones that he'd handpicked.

"Thanks for all your help," he said, turning his head slowly, making sure he made eye contact with everyone who had come in to help. "Jodie, what else needs to be done?"

"Nothing we can handle tonight," she said. "The insurance adjuster will be here first thing tomorrow. They suggested we hire a guard, and I called the security company. The guy is already in the parking lot."

"Let's lock up and go home." He found Angela watching him, and she smiled when he caught her glance. Jasper stayed in the heel position as they crossed the room. Angela handed him the leash, which he hooked onto the dog's collar.

With a chorus of goodbyes around them, they headed outside where dusk had fallen and the temperature had dropped to freezing.

"That's a nice group of people," Angela said to him after they were under way.

"They like you, too," he said.

"I made some calls about your dishes while I was waiting," she said. "Nordstrom has the pattern, and they're in stock." In the dim light, all he could make out of her was a silhouette, but he still felt a charge of awareness when she turned her head and looked at him. "Park Meadows Mall is more or less on the way back to your house."

"I doubt this is how you planned to spend your day," he said.

"That goes both ways. Do you want to go get the dishes?"

He laughed. "Single-minded has nothing on you, does it?"

"No," she said.

"Okay," he said.

On the way, he responded to Angela's questions

about the work of the Beanstalk Gang and the staff members she had met today. Since the work was his passion, he liked sharing, but he realized he wasn't learning anything new about her.

Dusk had fallen, and as always happened to Brian at night, what little vision he had left was a sea of black interspersed with the blurred lights of moving cars. Tonight, though, he studied Angela instead of closing his eyes against the kaleidoscope outside the car. She didn't seem to mind his looking at her because every time she turned her head toward him, she smiled.

He could get used to this, he thought. He wasn't sure how this woman had become so important to him over the space of a few days, but she had.

To his surprise, she found a parking place next to the store entrance when they arrived at the mall. When they got out of the car, he took her hand, like he had when they had arrived at the offices hours earlier.

She walked close enough to him that he sensed when they reached the curb without her saying anything. And when they entered the brightly lit store, he kept telling himself all the sensible reasons he had to hold her hand. It made maneuvering through the store easier. He wasn't likely to stumble over something hidden within the dark void of his nonexistent peripheral vision. The simple truth was, he liked it—from the scent of her hair to the clasp of her fingers against his. It felt…safe.

When they reached the china department, the choices turned out to be more complicated than he had imagined. Did he want a twelve-piece set or plates alone? Did he want the design with the gold rim or the platinum?

He'd never paid attention to that and had to take Angela's word that the rims of the broken plates were gold. Then they had added dessert plates and a coffee service. By the time they headed back to the car, Brian felt as though he had just finished playing a tough game with a rival team rather than simply shopping. He thanked the sales person who helped them carry the packages back to the Escalade and stow them in the back while Jasper watched attentively on from the backseat.

"Thanks to you, my grandmother is going to be a happy woman," Brian told Angela, holding the driver's door open for her. "I felt exactly like the proverbial bull in a china shop."

"You did just fine," she assured him. "Most guys would prefer a sporting-goods store over shopping for china."

He'd been referring to his sight loss, but she had seen his comment simply as one of those inexplicable differences between men and women. He looked down at her, close enough that her face was all he could see, her usual serene smile in place and her lips slightly parted.

He lowered his head, giving her time to back away if she wanted. She didn't, so he kissed her, cherishing the soft texture of her lips against his. She kissed him back before drawing away, her eyes impossibly bright when she opened them. He touched her cheek with a finger…and became aware that someone was clapping.

He lifted his head, hating that he couldn't recognize the shadowy figure approaching them. He stepped in front of Angela, shielding her with his body.

"So you guys are just friends," the man said, his voice familiar.

"Tommy? You followed us here?" Outrage filled Angela's voice as she let go of Brian's hand and took a step toward the other man. "I told you to leave me alone! I'm sick of you popping out of the woodwork every time I turn around."

"You know what I want, doll face."

The name reeked of disrespect and condescension, and made Brian instantly angry. He took a step forward, crowding the smaller man, who backed away. "That's Miss London to you, bud. Show a little respect."

Tommy laughed. "She's two-timing you, you know. Saw her on a date myself."

"Following her then, too?" Brian answered softly. He wasn't prone to physical violence, but at the moment, he imagined flattening this whiny user. "She's given every indication she doesn't want you around. Shove off."

Tommy took a step back, jamming his hands in his pants pocket, his attention once more on Angela. "Maybe your boyfriend would like in on our deal."

"There is no deal. Never was. Never will be," she said. "If I find you following me again, I'll call the police—"

"And what?" he challenged. "This is a public parking lot, and I just happened to cross paths with my old friend Angela."

Angela looked up at Brian, her features drawn. "Are you ready to go?"

"Sure."

She got into the car, putting the key in the ignition.

Brian closed the door and walked around the back of the car where he could still see Tommy's shadowy figure.

"Maybe I should come talk to *you* about my business proposition."

"No."

"C'mon. You don't even know what it's about. I watched what was going on over there at your offices. You're clearly a man who likes to dance on the shady side of the law."

NINE

Brian grabbed Tommy by his shirt front and pulled him close. "You don't know anything about me or my foundation." He gave the man a little shake. "Maybe you don't think Angela will call the police, but trust me, I will."

"And I'll tell them you assaulted me." Tommy grinned, his shoulders thrust back. "Go ahead, hit me. Make yourself feel like a man."

Brian was too tempted, even as something his grandfather had always said about heavy stones and a fool's wrath being even heavier flickered through his mind. Still, Brian couldn't release Tommy. "Leave Angela alone."

"Staking your claim?" Tommy pulled out of his grasp and straightened his coat. "Trust me. She's a woman without any staying power. Where she's concerned… if I were you, I'd be watching my back." With that, he walked away.

Brian got into the car. Once, he would have taken Tommy up on his taunt and flattened him without a backward glance. Brian shook his head against the conflicting emotions punching at him from inside his chest. Anger at a bully. Jealousy that any other man might have a claim on Angela. Pleasure at the memory of her sweet kiss. Swallowing, he turned his head to look at her.

Within the dark car, he couldn't see her expression as she started the engine and backed out of the parking place. For the first time, the silence between them was awkward rather than companionable. He couldn't decide if it was because of the kiss—hoping it wasn't, because he couldn't regret kissing her—or because of Tommy. Getting the man out of his mind was like trying to get away from the lingering stench of a skunk.

"Do you have big plans for Thanksgiving?" he asked, grasping on to the most neutral topic he could think of and knowing that he was going to invite her to spend it with his family if she said she didn't.

"Actually, I do." Her voice warmed, and he envied whomever she was spending it with. "For the first time in years, I'm having dinner with my friend Rachel and her family. Maisey is coming with me, too, and it's going to be great."

Rachel. Not a man. Brian couldn't deny that he was relieved even as Tommy's taunts rattled inside his head.

The rest of the drive was taken up with chitchat about the upcoming holiday that was only a couple of days away, the planned commercial shoot on Brian's schedule tomorrow morning and the training for Jasper that needed to be rescheduled. Little by little, the confrontation with Tommy faded.

By the time they pulled into the spacious garage next

to his grandparents' Buick, the mood between them had returned to its usual companionable one. Lights came on, illuminating the space.

"You've got to come in and meet my grandparents," he said as they got out of the car. "Plus, I want them to meet Jasper."

Angela chuckled. "And I thought the real reason was you wanted help carrying all these packages into the house."

"An added bonus," he agreed, meeting her at the back of the vehicle where they each picked up a couple of shopping bags. "Come on, Jasper. You're going to like Nonnie, and Gramps will probably think you're okay, too." After they opened the door into the house, he called, "I'm home."

Curious about his grandparents and far too consumed by thoughts of the kiss, Angela followed him down the hallway. The kitchen was brightly lit and filled with the aroma of something roasting. Breakfast had been hours ago, and she just now realized they had missed lunch. Her stomach growled.

Brian's grandmother and another woman were at the counter. Brian set his packages on the table, then reached for the ones in Angela's arms.

"Nonnie, this is Angela London," he said, drawing Angela toward a white-haired, dark-eyed woman whose face lit in welcome. "My grandmother, Priscilla Ramsey."

Drying her hands on a towel, she came toward them with a smile, her hands outstretched. "It's so nice to meet you. You wouldn't believe all the nice things that

Brian has said about you." She gestured toward the other woman. "This is Olivia Inness. Brian hired her to cook for us, which was a fortunate thing for me because otherwise we would have never met or gotten to be such good friends. Now then." She slipped behind Angela, pulling her coat from her shoulders as she spoke. "You need to take off your coat because you'll be staying for dinner, of course."

"Of course," Olivia agreed, while Brian said, "You might as well say yes right now because there will be no changing her mind."

"My grandson is right," Nonnie said, handing Angela's coat to Olivia, who carried it to the coat closet near the laundry room. Nonnie's gaze lit on Jasper, who was sitting next to Brian, and her smile grew even wider. "This is your dog. My! What a handsome boy he is." She looked over her shoulder to Angela. "Thank you for bringing him. I've been asking Brian for the last week when we were going to meet his French poodle." She came to a stop in front of the dog. "Why, look at you!"

Jasper's tail thumped, but he remained sitting at Brian's feet.

"He knows how to play, doesn't he?"

"Release," Brian commanded, grinning at Angela, who felt her stomach quiver the way it always did when she imagined that smile was meant only for her. With that, Jasper moved away from Brian, following Nonnie, who retrieved a box of dog treats from a pantry shelf. The dog's tail wagged harder.

Brian looked in Angela's direction. "Let the spoiling begin. She bought the dog treats the day after I announced I had found a dog."

She chuckled while Nonnie said, "This isn't spoiling. It's appreciation."

Angela's attention remained on Brian. This was a man she could fall in love with if she wasn't careful. And no way could she allow that to happen. All she had to do was look around the kitchen, which was nearly as big as her whole house, if she wanted a reminder of the gulf between them. And, if that didn't do it, she'd do well to think of her checkered past, which wasn't as far behind her as she had hoped. Brian Ramsey and his foundation didn't need the kind of baggage she carried.

On the other side of the room, Nonnie told Jasper to sit. He immediately did, earning his treat. After gushing over the dog a moment, Nonnie straightened, her smile brilliant.

"He's quite something, isn't he?" Brian said.

"Oh, yes." She came toward him, hugging him as though doing so was the most natural thing in the world. "I am so grateful for this answer to my prayers."

"That's what Angela said, too."

"Well, she's right." Nonnie turned her head, including Angela in her warmth.

"I've got a confession, Nonnie," Brian said, dipping his head, his expression suddenly contrite. "I had a little accident when I was getting your Christmas dishes down this morning."

Nonnie shook her head, her smile slipping a little. "I saw what was in the garbage. That looked like more than a little accident. Are you okay?"

"Fine." He gestured toward the packages. "I know it can never be exactly the same since you had been collecting the others. But, thanks to Angela, I went shopping and replaced the dishes."

"All of them?" She looked around Brian to the bags on the table.

"All of them," he said, dropping a kiss on her cheek. "Plus that coffee service that you've been talking about for a while."

"You didn't have to—"

"Yeah, I did."

"You shouldn't have—"

"I wanted to."

"It's too much money," Nonnie said.

"Not for you. Never for you," he said.

As Angela watched the interplay between them, she knew Brian had been given all the love and security possible while he was growing up. That he had it now. The fact that Nonnie had been concerned for him instead of the broken dishes said everything about the kind of woman she was. Angela hoped Brian knew how blessed he was.

He knew what it was like to be part of a loving and supportive family. She didn't. The feeling that flowed through her chest wasn't envy exactly, though she admitted wanting what he had. Loss, that's what it was, she decided. A sense of grief for something she'd never had.

Just then, a tall, white-haired man with Brian's chiseled features came into the kitchen. Undoubtedly this was Brian's grandfather. His face lit for the barest instant when he saw Brian, then settled back to a more somber expression.

"Wasn't sure whether you'd be back for supper or not," he said, his voice gruff. "That message you left on the phone worried your grandmother, you know."

"I'm sorry. There's not a real tactful way to describe vandalism." As Brian had done when he introduced Angela to his grandmother, he took her by the hand and brought her forward. "Angela, this is my grandfather, Philip Ramsey."

She extended her hand. "It's nice to meet you, sir."

He smiled, the somber expression vanishing completely, his warm welcome matching Nonnie's. "You're too pretty to be a dog trainer."

"And, Gramps, this is Jasper," Brian said while his grandmother said, "What a thing to say to the girl, Philip."

"Well, she is pretty." He turned around to look at the dog. "He's a poodle, all right." Glancing at Angela, he added, "You're sure this is going to work out? In my day the only Seeing Eye dogs you ever did see were German shepherds. Never heard of a poodle doing the job. It's sure a sissy-looking dog."

"Using poodles is a little unusual," Angela agreed, "but I found several case studies of poodles used in Europe, and a few here in the United States. I've spoken with a couple of the trainers and one of the owners. Poodles do extremely well at this work." She couldn't decide what to make of Brian's grandfather as his smile dissolved into the stern facade he'd worn when he first came into the kitchen.

"Brian seems to think it's okay, but I sure can't imagine such a thing," he said. A dismissal of sorts since his attention turned to Brian, and his expression became even more stern. Gramps nodded in the direction of the back hallway. "Come with me," he commanded Brian.

"Is this about the dishes, Gramps?"

"You know it is." His voice held a note of surprise though the glower stayed firmly in place.

"It's handled."

"You made your grandmother cry."

Brian's shoulders drooped. "I figured as much."

"I'm over it," Nonnie said from the stove where she lifted the lid on one of the pots and stirred whatever was inside. "He replaced them, Philip, down to the last saucer."

Gramps's gaze lit on the boxes of dishes that Olivia and Nonnie had taken out of the shopping bags. "Well. You should have been more careful." He looked at Brian. "New isn't necessarily better."

"No, sir, it's not."

"And just because you have money—"

"Let it go, Philip," Nonnie said, her voice mild, but the command unmistakable.

Another long glance passed between Brian and his grandfather, leaving Angela with the impression that Brian would do just about anything to earn his grandfather's approval. She also had the feeling that, despite his gruff tone and even gruffer demeanor, Philip Ramsey was proud of Brian. Finally, Gramps clamped a hand around Brian's shoulder in a gesture of support without saying anything further.

That telling moment brought a lump to Angela's throat, and she looked away only to find Nonnie watching her. She smiled and put Angela to work setting the table. The next few minutes were taken up with normal evening activities, reminding Angela just how lonely and quiet her own life had become. This was a family, including Olivia. Their sense of belonging to one another touched Angela at her deepest core, a feeling that intensified as Gramps said grace right after they sat down.

The prayer surprised her since Brian had hinted that he didn't attend church and was openly questioning his faith. As she thought about the things she had seen in his home today—the Nativity scene outside, the cross and welcome plaque near the garage door that was inscribed with a blessing from Isaiah for all who passed through—and in the man himself, she was fairly certain his grandparents had a deep reservoir of faith. She knew from personal experience just how difficult it was to hold on to one's belief in God during tough times, especially the core of Jesus's teachings about God's infinite love. Maybe that was part of what made Brian so intriguing, she thought. His journey of doubt reminded her of her own. And, since she'd found peace within her own faith, she could only hope he'd find the same.

She expected to feel like an outsider, but Nonnie and Gramps both kept the conversation focused on the activities surrounding Jasper's training and how the dog should be incorporated into their home life. Despite Gramps's often tough tone, it was obvious to Angela that he was both proud of Brian and deeply concerned about the changes that would ensue with his sight loss. Their matter-of-fact discussion about it lacked any hint of sentimentality.

When the meal was finished, Olivia began clearing the table, declining all offers of help. Brian and Gramps unpacked the boxes of dishes, and Nonnie oohed and aahed over each one, her appreciation clearly evident. Once more, Angela found herself included, which dissolved her intent to leave as soon as the meal was over.

But an hour later, the new dishes were all washed and put away, and she no longer had any reason to stay without overextending her welcome.

"I've got to go," Angela said.

"Already?" Nonnie asked.

"You'll come back soon?" Gramps said.

The genuine warmth in their voices made Angela smile as she extended her hand to each of them. "You'll probably see more of me than you want over the next few weeks as we finish up Jasper's training."

Nonnie hugged her. "You couldn't spend too much time," she said. "In case you don't know, you've been very, very good for my grandson. He's not as testy as he'd been lately."

"Nonnie," came Brian's warning tone.

Angela didn't look at him, but he sounded as though Nonnie had given away a secret he didn't want revealed. Once more, the memory of their kiss was right there at the surface, and she had another reason to avoid looking at him—her own discomfort.

Nonnie gave her a final squeeze. "See what I put up with? Testy." There was nothing but love in her voice or her expression as she looked from Angela to her grandson.

Waving, Angela headed for the back closet where she'd watched Olivia hang her coat earlier, murmuring her thanks for the meal and goodbyes as she went. Brian and Jasper followed her down the hall.

"You were great today. Thanks for all your help," Brian said, holding her coat so she could slip her arms into it.

"You're welcome." She liked the warmth in his voice. Too much. This time, her memory of the kiss included Tommy's interruption. Once more, she reminded herself she had no business getting involved with Brian. Snapping the leash on to Jasper's collar, she followed Brian into the garage where he hit the button for the door opener.

"I'm looking forward to the day when you can leave him here," Brian said. "When he's really mine."

"As soon as he passes his final trials, that will happen," Angela assured him, heading toward her car. She unlocked it and opened the back door, and Jasper climbed in. When she turned around, Brian was close, watching her with that intent way he had. "A couple more weeks, and he'll be all yours."

She knew he intended to kiss her, and she wanted him to.

"Angela," he murmured softly, dipping his head.

Closing her eyes, she put a hand against his chest and turned her face so his lips grazed her cheek.

"I can't do this," she whispered.

"Why not?" He lifted his head, and she met his gaze. "Are you involved with anyone else?"

"No." She took a breath and repeated, "No. But think. Everything about today is magnified. The accident with the dishes this morning and the break-in and… You're going through a lot, and all the stuff today just added to the stress level. That's all." That's all it could be, she thought, reminding herself that they were worlds apart in too many ways. She looked away from his penetrating gaze. "I know you're grateful for my help."

Grateful for my help. The words echoed in Brian's head, and he was instantly, unreasonably angry. What he felt for her had nothing to do with gratitude. But she was trying to put this thing between them in some tidy little corner where it could be labeled as gratitude or, even worse, pity.

She raised her head, and though the driveway was brightly lit, her face was hidden in shadows. She turned slightly, and he saw that her eyes were glistening, her expression reminding him of the day Erica walked out on him.

Angela looked back at him, her face once more hidden, the light illuminating her hair.

"Let's just chalk the feelings…and the kiss…up to the day, okay?" she said.

While he racked his brain for the right response to that, she got into her car.

A moment later, the motor came to life. She backed out of the driveway, and Brian remained standing there long after she was gone.

I know you're grateful. Chalk it up to the day. I can't do this.

Each one of those statements pulled tiny, painful chunks out of his heart. Going back into the garage, he turned off the exterior light, then pushed the button to close the door. If he looked carefully, he could see the dim bulb over the opener. Otherwise, the room was as black as the inside of his nightmare where the blind beggar and he became the same man.

TEN

"Cops are here to see you," Gramps told Brian the following afternoon, a few minutes after they had returned home from the commercial shoot.

Brian changed direction from the stairwell leading down to the workout room to the front of the house.

Late-afternoon sun poured through the windows of the foyer, illuminating the space and giving him halfway decent vision. He was expecting to see the detective who had been assigned to the vandalism case at the Beanstalk Gang. Instead, a pair of uniformed officers stood in the middle of the room.

Brian extended his hand, introducing himself, then asking, "What can I do for you?"

"You've been accused of an assault and we're here for the preliminary investigation," one of the officers, who had introduced himself as Officer Zander and his partner as Officer Quintin, said.

"What?" Brian shook his head. This wasn't about the break-in at the Beanstalk Gang offices?

"By a Thomas Manderoll," Quintin added. "Do you know him?"

"We've met," Brian said, Tommy's taunt to accuse him of assault flashing through his head. "Exactly what is he accusing me of?"

"Beating the tar out of him," Zander said, handing Brian a photograph.

Brian lifted it to the light. Despite the good light in the room, he couldn't focus clearly on the picture. He stared a long moment, then finally called to his grandfather, who came from the kitchen. Brian handed him the photograph. "What do you see?"

Gramps gave him a questioning look before taking the photograph and studying it. "A guy with a black eye and a cut over his eyebrow."

Brian took back the picture and looked at it again, frustrated that he couldn't make out any of the detail. He looked up in time to see an exchange of glances between the two officers. He wasn't ready to come clean with his sight loss and could imagine how strange his behavior must seem to them.

"I didn't do this," he said, handing the photograph back to Officer Zander.

"Even though, by your own admission, you can't see what 'this' is."

"I never hit the man, so if he looks like he has been, I didn't do it."

"And where were you last evening at six-thirty?" Quintin asked at the same moment that Gramps said, "I think I recognize this guy."

"From where?" Brian asked his grandfather. He didn't know Tommy Manderoll except in passing, but he was sure of one thing. He wanted the man nowhere near his grandparents.

"He came to the door a couple of days ago," Gramps replied. "Said he was selling magazine subscriptions." He looked at the officers. "Since this is a gated community and since there's not supposed to be any solicitation, I called security."

"Did you know about this?" Zander asked Brian.

"No." He had a good idea where that line of questioning was going—motive. "You asked where I was at six thirty last night. In the parking lot at Park Meadows Mall. He—" Brian pointed at the photograph "—was there, assuming that photo is of Tommy Manderoll."

"Maybe you'd like to relate what happened," Zander said while Gramps asked, "Do you need an attorney?"

Brian sighed. "The man evidently followed us—"

"Us?" Quintin interrupted.

Brian resisted rubbing the bridge of his nose. There was never anything such as a simple yes or no question. He should have remembered Angela's involvement before opening his mouth. On the other hand, if talking to the cops got Manderoll off her back...

"I was with Angela London. To be honest, Manderoll all but admitted to stalking her. I told him to back off, and he said he'd do as he pleased and threatened that he'd claim I'd assaulted him if I called the police."

"But you didn't do 'this,'" Zander said, tapping the photograph. "And Angela London will confirm it?" When Brian nodded, he added, "Do you have a phone number for her?"

"Only her work number," Brian said, reciting it to

them when Zander flipped open a notebook. He made a mental note to call her and let her know the police would probably be around asking questions.

After the officers left, Brian turned to his grandfather. "I want to know everything about what happened when that man came to the house. You didn't let him in, did you?"

Gramps stood taller and glowered. "Of course not. There's nothing to add. And there was no reason to think this had anything to do with you or your friend Angela." He started to walk away, then turned back. "You should call her. A man like that stalking a woman—"

Brian's throat closed with emotion as his imagination took off about that. Despite her assurances that she was handling Manderoll, Brian was beginning to think this was more serious than she was letting on. With that, he pulled out his cell phone and punched in the speed-dial for her number, leaving a message on her answering machine.

And he prayed for her safety, remembering her assertion that prayers were answered. This one deserved to be.

As the day wound down, he found himself thinking about their conversation about prayer being a way of aligning yourself to be in tune with God, a process that reminded him of the mental work required when playing with new guys on the team or adjusting to a new coach. The end result didn't change until the thinking did. And if he was understanding this faith thing right, the end result of his physical life wouldn't change much until his faith did. And so, he added a prayer to be less frustrated with his sight loss, feeling better despite also feeling awkward with the process.

"It's like old times," Rachel McLeod said to Angela.

"Yes," she agreed, rinsing off a serving bowl and setting it in the drainer.

They were washing the last of the Thanksgiving dishes in Rachel's spacious kitchen while the dishwasher hummed quietly. Like the rest of the hundred-year-old house in a historic Denver neighborhood near the Cherry Creek Mall, the kitchen had been remodeled, preserving the old architecture and adding modern amenities. Every detail showed Rachel's love and knowledge of antiques that had been incorporated into the house.

Angela looked over her shoulder toward the family room where Rachel's children, Sarah and Andy, were engaged in a spirited discussion about what television show to watch. Maisey, Reverend Chester, and Rachel's husband, Micah, were putting the extra leaves of the dining room table away. Jasper was curled up next to the ottoman in front of the couch, his watchful gaze following the children's movements.

This was a near perfect moment, Angela decided, since she was surrounded by people she loved. A woman couldn't ask for more than that.

"It really has been a day of thanksgiving, hasn't it?" Angela said.

"My thoughts exactly." Rachel swirled a towel around the inside of a serving bowl and set it down with others that needed to be put away. "If you had told me four years ago that life would be this good, I wouldn't have believed it."

Four years ago, Angela had been in prison, which hadn't been the worst of it. She had also been responsible for sinking the business she and Rachel had built together and leaving Rachel with a tattered reputation and no way to support herself. As often as Angela had been told that guilt was a futile emotion, she suspected she'd feel guilty about that for the rest of her life.

"I was so mad at you for the longest time," Rachel said, her voice soft. "And then I realized I hadn't been for a while. A *long* while, if I'm honest with myself."

Angela's hands stilled in the soapy water as she bowed her head and gripped the washcloth. "I—"

"Don't say anything." Rachel stepped so close, they were shoulder to shoulder, and Angela had the sense they were as they'd once been. Two ten-year-old girls joined at the hip and bound by the mutual deaths of their mothers and the recognition of a kindred spirit. "I'm not mad at you anymore. How could I be since that awful time set off a chain of events that brought Micah and a new beginning into my life?"

She stopped talking, and finally Angela looked at the woman who had been her best friend for twenty-five years. Rachel's eyes were bright with emotion.

"My dad believes the potential for good flows from everything, you know?"

Swallowing the lump in her throat, Angela nodded, her ears picking up the conversation beyond them and Reverend Chester's laugh.

"He's right," Rachel continued. "Look at all the good in my life that would have never come to me if—"

"I'm still sorry," Angela whispered.

"I know. But you and me, we're going to be okay." Rachel leaned forward until their foreheads touched. "Like we promised each other all that time ago—"

"Sisters and forever friends," Angela said, Rachel's voice joining hers with the last.

"You two look like you're plotting something," Reverend Chester said, coming up beside them and setting a coffee cup on the counter next to the sink.

Once, their plots had included dying their hair pink to match a favorite pop singer. Later the plotting had included their lives as adults—Rachel's wedding and later the funeral for her husband, and later still their decision to go into business together. Fun times, sweet times and bitter times.

As Angela considered that, she decided that Rachel might be on to something. Her life wouldn't be this full, this rich, if it hadn't taken the turns that it had.

"Nothing much has changed, then, has it, Dad?" Rachel said, moving away and opening cupboard doors to put away the serving pieces.

"Fortunately, no," he said, his kind gaze remaining on Angela. "Not the important things."

Micah and Maisey came into the kitchen, and Micah clapped his hands together. "Since the kitchen is cleaned up, it must be time to make turkey sandwiches."

"If I ate another bite, I'd explode," Rachel said, while Maisey said, "I ate too much already."

"I know what the real reason we eat so much on

Thanksgiving Day is," Andy said, sliding across the floor in his stocking feet. "It's getting all fueled up so we can go Christmas shopping tomorrow." He tilted his head back and looked at Micah. "There's a lot of stuff to look at in the toy store, don'cha think?"

"Just looking?" Micah teased.

"Yep," Andy said, opening the refrigerator door and grabbing a handful of carrots before skipping back into the family room. "Then I can make my list."

"He's planning," Maisey said with a chuckle.

Angela drained the water out of the sink and wiped the soap scum off the sides of it. Micah caught her eye, nodding toward the living room as though he remembered that she had wanted to talk.

"What's on your mind?" he asked when they reached the living room.

Beyond the windows, fat, lazy snowflakes were falling, illuminated by the street light, an idyllic contrast to Tommy's foundless accusation against Brian and constant, irritating presence in her life.

Since Micah had been the Special Agent in charge of the DEA investigation that had sent her to prison, if anyone had a good idea of how to deal with Tommy Manderoll, he would. She looked from the falling snow to a man she had once considered an enemy, realizing this was another of those déjà vu moments and remembering the frantic calls she had made to him from prison after she'd found out that Rachel was in danger. They had both moved on—he'd fallen in love with Rachel and now had a desk job at the DEA headquarters in

Denver, and she had a new life that she liked far more than her old one.

"I need some advice on dealing with Tommy Manderoll," she said, then related his demands for money, what had been going on over the last couple of weeks, and ending with his accusation that Brian had assaulted him.

In the middle of her relating the story, Micah sat down, watching her, his fingers steepled in front of his lips, his expression thoughtful.

"Do you think he's dealing?" Micah asked when she was finished.

She nodded, sinking into a chair across from him. "Tommy keeps alluding to some big deal he has going. He left a packet with me—taunted me with it, if you want the truth—evidently figuring I'd be open to his schemes if I was hooked again."

"What did you do with the drugs?"

Though his voice had no hint of accusation, she made sure she was looking at him when she said, "Flushed them down the toilet."

Micah nodded. "Probably a good choice, but the evidence would have been nice to have."

"That kind of evidence..." Angela shook her head against the memory of all the heartache her involvement with drugs had brought to people she loved. "I don't need it, don't want it."

"I know that. And it's okay." He reached for her hand. "Don't worry about Manderoll. Whatever he's got going, we'll figure it out and deal with it. Just keep me in the loop, okay?"

They talked a bit longer about Tommy, and if he'd

said where he was spending his time. She didn't know much at all, but Micah assured her that his people would know where to look. When they rejoined the others, Angela felt as though a weight had been lifted from her shoulders, for which she gave a silent prayer of thanks.

On one hand, she hadn't wanted to bother Micah with the problem. But then she remembered what she'd said to Brian about God working for us by working through us. That was, she decided, advice to trust, and Micah's promise for help proved it.

An hour later, she arrived at home after dropping Maisey off at her house. The telephone was ringing when she and Jasper came through the door. The caller ID showed Brian's cell phone number.

"Hi, Brian," she said, glad to hear from him and putting aside her nearly constant admonishment that she couldn't get involved with him beyond Jasper's training. "How was your Thanksgiving?"

"How'd you know it was me?" he asked.

"Caller ID." She took off her coat and sat down on the couch, curling her feet under her.

"Ah. Thanksgiving was fine. Actually, what I was calling you about—I need a rescue."

She looked outside at the falling snow. "You're stranded? Where are you?"

He laughed. "No, not stranded. I'm at home. Actually…"

His voice faded away, and such a long moment of silence followed that she wondered if the call had been disconnected.

"Are you still there?" she finally asked.

"Yeah. Actually, I was wondering if you might be available to go with me to a silent auction this Friday. My buddy Oliver Kamenski—he plays with the Avalanche, you know—sponsors this annual fund-raiser to buy sports equipment for kids and since the Beanstalk Gang is one of the beneficiaries, I always go."

The rush of words faded away, and Angela felt her heart pound. The rescue was a date? Every fiber of her being told her this was a bad idea. She sometimes read the society pages, and she knew this was the kind of event that was covered by the media, which meant photographers and reporters.

"Please," he said. "You'd be doing me a huge favor."

"Huge, hmm?" Despite her reservations, the plaintive tone made her chuckle.

"Huge," he agreed, his voice filling with relief. "You have no idea."

"I suspect there are a lot of women in Denver who would go with you," she said.

"Maybe. But with the exception of Jodie and the others at the Beanstalk Gang, nobody knows I'm going blind."

The bubble of elation that she was somehow special enough to be his date for such an event popped. Of course. He needed someone on his arm who could guide him through the maze of a banquet room.

"I'd be happy to rescue you," she said, lapsing into her professional voice and irritated with herself that she had wanted something more. This was business, just like she wanted.

"Great." Brian reached out to touch the cold glass

of the window of his bedroom. Beyond it, the night was just as black as the inside of his room where he hadn't yet turned on a light. It had been snowing when he'd been outside earlier, but he couldn't see it, though he imagined the faint light from other windows in the house making the flakes shimmer. Thinking about that was easier than his deliberate ploy to play on Angela's professional sympathy. After professing to himself that he didn't want her pity, this was beyond lame.

The truth was he wanted to take back trying to coerce her into going because of his sight loss. The truth was that he wanted her to go with him simply to be together, not because she felt sorry for him or saw it as some duty foisted onto her.

"Do you want me to meet you or come to your house?" she asked.

He cleared his throat. "Sam will be driving. We'll pick you up at six-thirty." The moment to take back the invitation was gone. Pity or not, he was glad that she'd agreed to go.

ELEVEN

Her hand tucked in the crook of Brian's arm, Angela felt a bit like a princess out of a fairy tale. She glided with him down the wide, graceful staircase that ended in a brightly lit atrium outside the large ballroom. A few partygoers, all decked out in their best holiday finery, were gathered at the doorway. In the center of the group stood a tall, athletic-looking man wearing a white tuxedo with tails, a bright red cummerbund and a red top hat. Laughter and Christmas carols wafted from inside the room.

They reached the bottom of the stairs where Brian came to a stop. When she looked up at him, he was watching her so seriously that she had to ask, "Are you okay?"

While they had been training Jasper yesterday, he had told her that his sight had reduced to such a degree that he felt as though he were looking through a straw. At the time, she had expected him to be more dejected, but he'd been matter-of-fact, just as he'd been any time his sight loss came up. The one exception had been that day in his kitchen. He'd been in her prayers since then asking, among other things, that he find his way toward God where he'd also find comfort.

"Great," he said, returning her attention to the present. "Plus, the prettiest woman here is with me."

"You can't know that." She felt her cheeks heat. "We haven't been inside yet."

"I know that," he insisted.

"Thank you." She wished his thinking she was pretty wasn't so important to her. "You clean up pretty well, yourself."

That was an understatement. His black tux made him look as though he'd stepped off the cover of *GQ*. She was proud to be with him.

What a heady thing this was. Brian's attention and care to detail had begun with the gorgeous wrist corsage he'd given her when he had picked her up. She had resolved she wouldn't get carried away. This was business, since he had used his sight loss as the reason for her to accompany him. Just business.

She caught a whiff of the roses in the corsage, their crimson color nearly the same shade as the cranberry pashmina she had splurged on to give her plain black silk dress some holiday flair. Carried away? Oh, but she was. A Cinderella at the ball, expecting the clock to strike midnight at any moment.

"Shall we do this?" He squeezed her hand and winked at her.

"We've come this far," she murmured.

He laughed, his tension gone, at least for the moment, and led her toward the group gathered in front of the ballroom door.

"Brian, it's great to see you," said the man in the white tuxedo, his French-Canadian accent filled with pleasure. "One of the joys of retirement, no? You can be here with a pretty woman on a Friday night instead of preparing for the big game." He shook Brian's hand, then let it go, taking Angela's and smoothly continuing, "You, lovely lady, can do so much better than this man."

Brian reclaimed Angela's hand and introduced the man as Oliver Kamenski, then added, "Don't let the accent fool you. Ollie is—"

"Charming," Oliver said while Brian said, "Dangerous."

Angela laughed. "I can see you're both right."

"A diplomat," Oliver said. "And a pretty one." He slapped Brian on the back, pointing them toward the expansive ball room. "I will talk to you later, my friend, after you have opened your checkbook and spent all your money."

In contrast to the bright atrium, the lights of the ballroom were turned down to enhance the decorations, which were tasteful and lush. Items up for auction were expertly illuminated. A jazz quartet in one corner provided live music, loud enough to add to the festive flair, soft enough that people didn't have to shout over the music.

"This is as dark as a tomb," Brian grumbled next to her.

She squeezed his hand. "Actually, it's beautiful. It looks like a Victorian Christmas." Looking around, she softly said, "A gorgeous blonde is making a bee-line toward us."

"Brian," the woman called, her smile as bright as her voice. "Oliver said I'd just missed you, so I had to come looking." She kissed him on the cheek, then offered her hand to Angela. "I'm Thea Kamenski. Did this lug tell you that he's the first person we met when we arrived in town?"

"He didn't," Angela admitted.

"This is Angela," Brian said.

"It was right after he bought that wonderful house of his and the only furniture was a sixty-inch big-screen TV. We all camped out on the floor in sleeping bags and had a grand time. It's nice to see Brian dating again." Her gaze lit on someone coming toward them, then she gave Angela air kisses on each cheek. "There's Larry and his wife. I've gotta run. We'll talk later."

Angela looked back at Brian, Thea's statement echoing between them. Dating *again?*

As if discerning her thoughts, he said, "I suppose it would be very bad form right now to tell you I'd been engaged until a few months ago."

If they had been romantically involved, he was right. But, since this was business... Except, she finally acknowledged, it didn't feel like business. She hadn't had butterflies like these in forever. And no date had ever been more attentive than Brian was being right now. Worse, she had no idea what to say to put herself and him at ease.

"Anyway, it's over." He handed her the program he'd been given when they came into the ballroom. "You can help me decide what to bid on."

That didn't sound quite like a man who was glad

that his engagement was broken, which left her wondering about the nameless fiancée. She had no time to dwell on that, however, since a distinguished-looking man was greeting Brian. She missed his name in the introduction, but gathered that he was the president of the National Milk Association. He and Brian chatted a moment before they all moved on.

They traded pleasantries with numerous people from the entire spectrum of Denver's elite—wealthy businessmen, professional athletes, a hometown entertainer and elected officials, including a U.S. senator. As they wandered around the room, Brian kept hold of her hand, introducing her as though she was important to him. His generous inclusion of her made it too easy to imagine she wasn't simply visiting his life, she was part of it.

He passed right over the sports memorabilia display, but not before she caught a glimpse of his donation to the cause, an autographed football and helmet in a display case. After Brian told her he wanted to find a piece of glass art for his grandmother, Angela began pointing those out for him. By the time they had completed the circle and been guided toward the seating for the banquet, he had written down bids for several pieces. Included in his bids was a large vase that contained exquisite glass flowers imbedded within the design. Another item was a glass poodle prancing through a cobalt-blue paperweight. Each object was worth thousands of dollars.

They had just sat down when Angela looked up to see Andrew Brogg advancing on them with a photographer in tow.

"Mind if we get a photo?" he asked, motioning for the photographer to take the picture before they could respond.

"You remember Andrew Brogg," Angela said, since the man hadn't stayed in one spot long enough for Brian to focus on him.

"He remembers me," Andrew said tightly. The hostility in his tone made Angela look more closely at him.

"Nice to see you, too," Brian said with a slight nod.

She had been around Brian enough to recognize his game face—the mask he wore when being in control was everything to him.

Andrew pulled out the chair next to Brian and sat down. "Anything for the record?"

"Oliver Kamenski has put on a great event and I hope he raises a lot of money," Brian said.

Andrew leaned closer. "I was talking about the charges of assault that Tommy Manderoll filed against you. Anything to say about that?"

The only sign of tension in Brian was an imperceptible tightening of his fingers around hers. The venom in Andrew's tone had Angela baffled. He acted as though Brian had somehow personally offended him, though neither of them had given her a bit of indication they were acquainted. Clearly, they were.

When Andrew looked at her, she realized that hostility was also directed at her. "Now why would an ex-boyfriend of yours be tangled up with your new boyfriend? It's one of those stories that ought to be on the front page of a tabloid."

"That's where you usually find the lies." Brian's tone, like his expression, was bland.

Angela waved a hand. "That whole thing of interviewing me for a feature about Guardian Paws—"

"There will still be a feature." Andrew looked at Angela, then back at Brian, nodding as though he'd figured out something. "You know, I just keep connecting the dots. Here's your new boyfriend, the one who evaded rumors for years about supplying steroids to his teammates. And then, there's that kid who was arrested a few weeks back for peddling drugs before it was all hushed up and swept under the rug. What was his name?"

Angela had the feeling Andrew knew, but he was clearly enjoying his little drama.

He snapped his fingers. "Oh, yeah. Ivan Fletcher, the kid who spends all his time at the Beanstalk Gang. Now, I can't help but wonder if he had anything to do with the vandalizing of your place last week. Any comment about that?" His sharp gaze returned to her. "And then there's your ex-boyfriend, and if there ever was a junkie he surely is."

Angela felt ice replace the blood in her veins and her lips go numb at the mention of Tommy. Andrew was right. Tommy *was* a junkie, but how could Andrew have known that?

"I think you're done here," Brian softly said, steel lacing his voice.

"Not quite." Andrew's gaze hardened, pinning her in her chair until he looked back at Brian. "Did you know Angela and I had dinner a couple of weeks ago? A nice one, too. Of course, my pockets aren't as deep as yours."

Stung by the accusation, Angela said, "You know that was a business meeting—"

"Do I?" He shrugged, then stood. "I don't usually ask the subjects I'm interviewing to dinner. And you told me that you weren't dating Ramsey, but here you are, holding hands."

When she would have pulled hers away, Brian's grip tightened.

"Like I said, you're done here," Brian said.

"And if I'm not, you'll take care of me the same way you handled Tommy Manderoll?" Andrew stood and carefully slid the chair back under the table. "I have to hand it to you, Angela. You must be something to have Ramsey and Manderoll both fawning over you." When Brian surged from his chair, Andrew grinned and stepped back. "No need for the caveman act. I'm going."

A thousand thoughts churned in Angela's head as Brian sat back down, once more taking her hand as if to reassure them both. Andrew knew Brian and, for some reason, clearly hated him. And she'd been a pawn to get closer to Brian. She had no doubt that Andrew was working on a feature, but instead of appearing in the Family Living section of the paper, he was aiming for something bigger.

Her drug-related conviction, Tommy's intrusion into her life and the troubles with the Beanstalk Gang had undoubtedly provided Andrew with the dots he'd mentioned. It didn't take a genius to figure out that he was trying to prove they were involved with drugs.

The whole thing made her head pound. The sweet butterflies that had been in her stomach earlier were now replaced with a swarm of wasps stinging the inside of her chest. Would she never be free of her past?

On that thought, she looked up and found Brian's gaze on her.

"Brogg has been on my tail for months. Anything he said to rattle you was to get a rise out of me."

Much as Angela appreciated that Brian was trying to reassure her, she was positive her conclusion was right. Given Andrew's dislike of Brian and her own felonious past, why wouldn't Andrew think they were selling drugs? The only thing she was positive about was that any involvement with her could only spell trouble for Brian's work with the Beanstalk Gang.

She couldn't do that to Brian.

She met his gaze once more, and he smiled. "I don't believe a word of what he said about you, you know."

"I know," she somehow managed around the fear choking her. Remembering she'd felt like Cinderella when they had arrived, she knew the clock had struck midnight and the fairy tale was over. She *had* to make sure Brian wasn't hurt by any connection with her.

The thought broke her heart. She loved this man. How could she have been so blind not to have recognized it until this minute? Not once in her whole life had the flood of emotion been as strong as it was now. She wanted a life with him. More, she wanted what was best for him, and that wasn't her. A lifetime of images that would never be flashed in front of her, powerful in their loss.

Oh, God, she prayed. *Help me be strong enough to do what's right.*

* * *

"Got any more nose candy for me?" Andrew asked Tommy right after their coffee was delivered. They were sitting side by side at the counter of a diner a few blocks away from the Beanstalk Gang offices.

The effects of the beating that Ramsey had supposedly given Tommy were still evident, a purple and green bruise running along the length of his jaw line. Tommy looked at him sideways. "You know we're not gonna do that right here."

Andrew nodded. "I know. I just need to know you've got it." He hoped he'd placed the right inflection in his voice to sound needy, like he was worried about withdrawal.

Christmas carols played through the sound system, and silver garland had been hung on the wall across from them. Next to him, Tommy fidgeted, and when he looked at Andrew, his pupils were pinpoints. For the kind of information Andrew wanted, it would have been better if Tommy hadn't been strung out—it would be easier to convince his editor that his information was accurate if his source was sober. But, on the other hand, since he was high, Andrew could play that to his advantage. The other time he'd met with Tommy, the man had been full of himself, bragging about his connections and his big plans. What Andrew wanted was for Tommy to implicate Ramsey. And now that Andrew knew Angela was their likely go-between, that was looking more positive by the minute.

Tommy took a sip of his coffee, his attention on the pie display behind the counter. "Yeah, I've got it." When the waitress came back, he said, "I'd like a piece of that cherry pie. With ice cream."

After she had served Tommy and moved away, Andrew cleared his throat. "That deal you were telling me you had going with Angela London—how's that coming along?" So far, Andrew had only Tommy's word that Angela was bankrolling some big deal that he had going. Tommy hadn't been subtle about the deal—he was setting up a distribution network, and he had his eye on the Beanstalk Gang. Since Andrew was convinced Ramsey was using the place as a front, he figured Tommy was simply a small-time player who wanted to be something more. If it helped Andrew prove his case, he was happy to let Tommy think he was the one pulling the strings. If he could just get the man to give him some cold, hard facts, not just innuendo...

Tommy polished off the pie and took another sip of coffee before looking at Andrew. "You asking as a reporter or..."

He shrugged. "Just want to make sure I can depend on you for the stuff." Andrew turned his gaze inward to make sure he wasn't making eye contact with Tommy. In actual fact, Andrew had never used and never would. However, making Tommy think that he did was worth it if it nailed Ramsey. Plus, there was the matter of Angela London. He didn't buy her woman-reformed act, convincing as she had tried to be.

"I saw her last night at a big shindig downtown," Andrew added. "And she was on Brian Ramsey's arm. She didn't look much like a woman with business on her mind, if you know what I mean."

Tommy was silent for a moment, then turned to Andrew with a gleam in his eye. "She's just doing her thing. Working the rich crowd, just like she's been doing for me for years. You should have seen her in action when we were doin' Aspen a few years ago. She was something."

"So Ramsey is an investor in your—"

"He'll come around," Tommy said. "Angela will make sure of it." He swiveled on his stool so he was facing Andrew. "You're not asking all these questions for a story, are you? You're being on the up-and-up about wanting a reliable source for the stuff, right?"

Andrew nodded. "A reliable source. That's exactly what I've wanted all along."

TWELVE

"Good morning, Brian," said Maisey Erdmann when he came through the door of Guardian Paws on Monday morning.

"Hey, Maisey. It's pretty bright and early to see you," he returned. He rarely saw her at the facility when his training time with Angela was this early. All weekend, he'd been looking forward to seeing Angela, admitting to himself that she meant more to him than being his trainer. Granted, that meant ignoring her warning, the night of the break-in at the Beanstalk Gang, that they couldn't get involved. A man didn't get what he wanted without taking risks.

"Angela is waiting for you in her office. I'll see you in a few minutes."

Brian headed through the kitchen, following the aroma of freshly brewed coffee down the hallway to the bedrooms that had been converted into offices. Angela's was in the back overlooking the yard where the dogs in training were playing. Her back was to the door, and she was absorbed with her task at the computer.

He stood there a second just looking at her, happy to

be in her company. Somehow he had resisted calling her all weekend, though he'd made up a dozen reasons to do so. Like wanting to tell her that he'd gone to church with his grandparents yesterday. He'd wanted to share his thoughts about the sermon, which had been about being called to be of service even when you didn't feel worthy. The reverend had used Moses as an example. Brian was surprised—the only version of Moses he'd known about was the man who'd led the Israelites out of Egypt and had parted the Red Sea. He hadn't known the man had probably had a speech impediment. The story had touched his heart. If Moses could become eloquent enough to make a pharaoh listen to him, then surely Brian could do the work he'd set out for himself in helping kids, whether he was sighted or not.

Both Angela and Sam had shone a light on the path without pushing him, and this morning he was grateful and filled with renewed optimism that everything was going to be okay.

"Hey," he finally said.

She whirled around in her chair, her eyes wide with surprise.

"Sorry," he added. "I didn't mean to scare you."

Hues of pink pulsed from her neck to her hairline, and her surprised expression gave way to resignation.

"Everything okay?" he asked as she turned back to the computer where she pressed a button.

"We need to talk," she said, turning back around, her eyes not quite meeting his.

That didn't sound good.

"Then let me get some coffee, if we're not headed

right out." He went to the kitchen, worry dogging each step he took. *We need to talk.* Code for *There's deep trouble and you're not going to like it.*

Of all the words a guy never wanted to hear, those were close to the top of the list. She hadn't given him a smile or the cheerful "good morning" that she always did. He didn't know what, but something was wrong. He looked through the kitchen window above the sink that overlooked the yard, afraid suddenly that something had happened to Jasper. Maybe that was it.

Only a second later, Jasper bounded into his line of vision. One worry eased as Brian turned toward the coffeemaker and poured a cup.

When he returned to her office, she had moved from behind the desk to one of the side chairs. She briefly met his gaze when he came in, then looked away.

"Whatever's going on can't be as bad as all that." He set the cup on the corner of the desk and sat down on one of the chairs next to her.

She looked at him once more, and if her hands hadn't been locked together in her lap, he would have taken one of them and promised her things would be okay. Except he couldn't offer that since he had no idea what was on her mind.

"Angela?"

She took a breath. "Tell me about Andrew Brogg," she said.

"What?" Of all the questions she might have asked, that one hadn't even been on the radar.

"I've been thinking about the things he said the other night—"

This he could handle, Brian thought. "He was full of hot air, like always."

"Except that he has a venue to express his opinions. The other day when I told you he was watching you—I thought he was following me. But he wasn't, was he?"

"Probably not," Brian admitted. "He's got this theory he's trying to prove. Only, he can't because it isn't true."

"What theory?"

"Angela, I don't want to talk about him or this—"

"What theory?" she repeated, reaching out to touch the back of his hand, her own cold and clammy.

When she would have pulled her hand away, he clasped it in his larger, warmer one. "He's got this idea that I'm using the Beanstalk Gang to peddle drugs to kids." Brian closed his eyes, then stared at their clasped hands. "In his mind, there doesn't appear to be much of a leap between abusing steroids—and though I did, he can't prove it—and selling drugs." He looked at Angela. "The man is an irritation, but without facts—which he won't get because there aren't any. He's a blowhard, just like I said."

Her eyes shimmered and she shook her head, pulling her hand from his and wrapping it around her middle. "You're not so naive to believe that." Her gaze shifted and she stared out the window. "Now that I'm in the picture, he has reason to look harder."

"What are you talking about?"

"My prison time for—"

"Your what?" Her words clanged through Brian's head. Prison? Angela? That didn't make sense.

"You didn't know I'd been in prison?"

"No." His voice ground past the dry sand scratching the inside of his throat.

"You never checked out our website, or read the interview where I talked about how I came to be a dog trainer?"

"No." Brian rubbed his temple, his attention fixed on her.

"Oh, Brian," she whispered. "What a mess this is, and I am so, so sorry for it."

This conversation had gone from bad to horribly worse. "Maybe..." He cleared his throat, then said, "Maybe you should start at the beginning."

She laughed harshly, a sound so unlike her that he flinched. "The beginning." She surged from her chair and went to stand in front of the window, both her arms wrapped protectively around her. "I had prayed that part of my life was behind me," she said so softly he strained to hear her. "All I wanted was a fresh start."

She bowed her head a moment, and he wondered if she was praying or simply gathering courage and concentration since the gesture reminded him of his own mental preparation.

"You deserve to know all of it." She turned around and looked at him. "And then you'll know why I worry about Andrew Brogg."

He reached a hand toward her and motioned for her to sit next to him. "It can't be as bad as all that," he said, recognizing the words were an echo of what he'd told her earlier.

"You might be surprised." She sat down, staring at a point just beyond his shoulder, then said, "I used to be in business with my friend Rachel. We'd been best friends for years, and it was the perfect thing to match our talents—her knowledge of antiques and my connections with people with money. And about a year later I met Tommy Manderoll. At the time I thought he was charming, and he certainly was fun to be around. One thing led to another, and one night I found myself at a party with him where everyone…and I mean everyone…was partying with cocaine."

She fell silent, and Brian watched her, knowing what that party had been like because he'd seen a few of them himself. Because of his mother's problem with drug use, he'd never been remotely tempted, and he'd seen enough to know he'd been smart about that though he'd made his share of mistakes about other things.

"Anyway, I tried it, and from that moment, I did stupid things for reasons that don't even make sense to me anymore. The worst of those was using our business to launder drug money for a cartel that Tommy was involved with. The DEA came in, confiscated everything, and after Tommy made a deal and turned state's evidence, I was convicted of possession with an intent to sell and operating as a front for organized crime."

Her voice was emotionless, and that somehow ratcheted Brian's tension to near breaking. He couldn't get his head around everything she was saying to him, couldn't imagine her involved with the kinds of things she said she had done.

"But that wasn't the worst part. There was a reporter out to make a name for himself, and he did that by becoming judge and jury in the press. I deserved it. But he also vilified Rachel, who'd done nothing wrong except trust me. She was ruined, which I have to live with for the rest of my life," Angela said.

"Wasn't she the one you spent Thanksgiving with?"

Angela nodded, then took another deep breath. "I spent two years in prison, and the only good thing out of that was learning to train dogs."

"You said it was what you were meant to do." What he was fixated on, though, was the first part. *I spent two years in prison.* And related to the thing he hated most—drug use.

"It is. And I've come far enough since then to know that the person I am today is a result of all those experiences. But it doesn't mitigate my behavior or the rumors."

"Tommy wants you to go back into business with him," Brian stated.

"He does. But it will never, ever happen."

"How can you be so sure?" He asked the question softly. He'd been abandoned by a mother who had loved her drugs so much she hadn't wanted him. He'd never imagined that he'd be looking across that particular abyss again. And that told him just how deeply he had fallen for Angela.

"Because I'm a different person now than I was then." As was the usual for her, there was no rancor in her voice when she answered.

"That's when you got religion?" He knew just how derisive that sounded, wanted it to, in fact, since anger was beginning to simmer in his chest.

She didn't immediately answer, and when he raised

his gaze to her face, he found she was steadily watching him, the sadness in her eyes so deep that he wanted to take the words back.

"Yes," she said, "it was. There's nothing quite like being alone with your own morbid thoughts to bring you face-to-face with your Creator. But that's not the point right now." She dropped her head as if composing her thoughts. "When Andrew showed up for the feature he was supposedly doing on Guardian Paws, he asked dozens of questions about you. At the time I thought it was just because you were a celebrity. Then Tommy showed up and interrupted the interview, and that's when Andrew said he already knew about the relationship between Tommy and me. And the only way he could have found that out was if he'd read about it in the Aspen and Glenwood Springs papers or if Tommy had told him. I didn't know he was gunning for you until last Friday night."

She surged from the chair and went to stand in front of the window once more. And all Brian could do was watch, knowing that she was hurting but caught up in his own frustration and disappointment and furious that he was losing something that had been important to him.

"Jasper is a great dog," she said. "The right dog for you. We're nearly finished with the training, which Maisey can continue with you. And I can convince Andrew that I was only your trainer, nothing more, and try to minimize the damage to you and your foundation."

"You're going to lie?"

She shook her head and met his gaze. "No. It's the truth, Brian." Her chin quivered. "I never want to see you again."

Brian sat there in shock after she swept out of the room, his brain hardened into some unrecognizable mass that felt like it would crumble into bits like old, dried bread if he so much as moved. When Maisey came to the door sometime later he couldn't have said if seconds or hours had passed.

"Let's get to work," she briskly said, nudging his shoulder.

He stood then, his heart crumbling into dust just as he had feared.

"You can sit here and feel sorry for yourself or you can get to work."

Hers was the mandate of coaches everywhere, but today there would be no blocking sleds or agility trainers to navigate to diffuse all this pent-up energy.

"I'm not feeling sorry for myself," he said.

"No? You could have fooled me. Anyone can see you've fallen in love with her, and she's just pulled the rug out from under you."

His heart pounded at that. How could Maisey know he was in love with Angela when he didn't know it for sure himself?

The rest of the day passed in a haze, none of it going well. Not the training time with Jasper. Not the usual Monday meeting with the Beanstalk Gang staff. Not the meetings with the insurance company, which was going to cover less than half the cost of repairing and replacing equipment that had been damaged or stolen in the break-in. It was all topped off with a report on the evening news, suggesting that Ivan Fletcher—the kid who had been arrested when his brother had sold drugs to an undercover cop a few weeks before—was a person of interest in the break-in at the offices. There had also been a veiled suggestion that the organization was a possible front for gang activity.

Brian's attorney called before the newscast ended, promising that he was already on it.

Brian headed up to his bedroom to change his clothes, sitting down on the bench in the middle of the closet to take off his shoes. Instead of doing so, though, he propped his elbows on his knees and rested his head in his hands. He felt as alone and forlorn as he had when he was six and facing that first night in his grandparents' home.

He hadn't known what to expect then, and right now wasn't a whole lot better.

Bits and pieces jumbled through his head, bouncing to things Angela had said and back to pieces of the sermon he'd heard the day before. He remembered sitting in church and feeling relief that he wasn't the agnostic he'd feared he was; he had faith. In that moment, he was sure that he was feeling the presence of God and, right now, he was just as sure it had all been an illusion. He was alone and in the dark, figuratively and literally, just as he had so often been before.

"Brian?" Gramps called.

Brian lifted his head and realized he was sitting in the dark.

His grandfather called again.

"In here," he said.

A second later he sensed Gramps at the doorway, and the lights went on. The straw through which Brian could see had grown smaller. Had it been that way all day, or was he just now noticing?

"I just came to tell you that Olivia is dishing up supper."

"I'll be down in a minute." He bent to take off his shoes, then felt Gramps sit down on the bench next to him.

"What are you doing, sitting up here in the dark?"

"Lights on or off," Brian said, "it's not making a lot of difference anymore."

"That's not what I meant."

"It's been a tough day, Gramps."

"Some are like that."

They sat shoulder-to-shoulder a moment longer. The conversation with Angela took hold of Brian's thoughts again and somehow became all mixed up in his mind with the sermon about Moses once being an ordinary man who was called to do extraordinary things.

"Why don't you tell me what's wrong instead of leaving me to fill in gaps for a story I don't know," Gramps said.

"That's a little hard with my thoughts going everywhere all at once." Brian closed his eyes, then opened them again. A tiny sliver of light was all that remained. "I keep thinking about the sermon yesterday—"

"That's good."

"And how we're called to service."

"That's usually how it works. Pay attention and God shows you the way."

"Do you really believe that?" Brian asked.

"I do." Gramps's voice became gravelly then, as he laid a hand on Brian's knee. "It's how I had the privilege of raising you."

Brian's eyes unexpectedly, inexplicably burned. "When I was a boy, I was scared of you."

"I know."

"Angela told me today that she'd been in prison."

"Was she, now?"

"For drug-related charges."

"I see." Gramps cleared his throat. "Guess that had you thinking of your mother some and the mess she made of things."

"Yep."

"Angela, she's nothing like that."

"I'd like to be sure."

"Ah, my boy. You know better than that. Only three things you can be sure of in this life. Death. Taxes."

When he didn't say anything for a moment longer, Brian asked, "And?"

"God's love." Gramps sighed. "Now that I look back on it, I know I didn't tell you often enough. Your grandmother and I love you. We're proud of you, you know."

Brian swallowed the enormous lump in his throat. He did know. And somehow, Gramps had figured out that he needed reassurance. For it to come on this day, when he felt under attack from all corners, meant everything.

"I know that, Gramps."

Gramps patted his knee. "Come on down for dinner before it gets cold."

"I'll be along in a minute," Brian promised as his grandfather ambled out of the room.

One of the things Angela had said earlier echoed through Brian now, and he had a flash of clarity that it was as true for him as it had been for her. *There's nothing quite like being alone with your own morbid thoughts to bring you face-to-face with your Creator.* In this moment, he finally understood the source of her calm since she'd also told him that she knew God's will could be only for good. If God loved him and if God's will was only for good, then somehow, there had to be a way out of the morass.

The first step was admitting that he'd judged her. He'd sat there like the hypocrite that he was, pretending to be superior and ignoring that his abuse of anabolic steroids was just as damning as anything she'd done.

The rest of what she'd said tumbled through his mind, and he realized she'd had a single focus—concern for him, about the fallout her situation had on him, and his work. Not once had she mentioned wanting to make sure she came out of this thing okay. As he thought it through, he realized his own tarnished past cast a shadow over her and the good that Guardian Paws did. How could he have been so smug, so sure that he stood on higher ground?

Oh, God. The thought was one of despair, but it was also the beginning of a prayer. "Help me see the next steps," he whispered. "Help me do what's right for Angela."

By the following morning, Brian had decided prayer was a bit like getting his head into a game before it started. The process was one of emptying his mind and opening it to the outcomes he intended, but this time trusting in God's will rather than his own. It was at once frightening and exhilarating. He couldn't have described the experience if his life had depended upon it, nor could he put his finger on exactly what had happened to him during the night, but he was sure of two things: God loved him, and as long he remained in that knowledge, he'd be okay.

He also knew what he had to do to disarm Brogg and the speculation in the media. Come clean with it all. His sight loss and his abuse of anabolic steroids.

Then, maybe, just maybe, he could protect Angela as completely as she seemed determined to protect him.

THIRTEEN

Two weeks before Christmas, Angela came out of the local animal shelter, discouraged. None of the dogs she'd looked at today had exhibited either the personality profile or obedience aptitude she was looking for. Lots of nice dogs that needed homes and would make great pets. Just none that suited her purposes.

Mentally crossing this shelter off her list, and thinking about the others she intended to visit in the two weeks remaining before Christmas, she headed across the parking lot. Maisey had accused her of running so she wouldn't risk bumping into Brian, and though Angela had denied it, she knew it was true. Everything reminded her of the man. Walking the familiar neighborhood in Brighton where she'd done the majority of Jasper's training. Driving around Denver and remembering all the different places she'd been with Brian.

Getting her keys out of her pocket, she looked up and found Tommy leaning against her car as though he had all day and as though the weather wasn't cold and gray enough to be spitting intermittent snow.

"You keep turning up like a bad penny," she said to him. "Go away."

The face she'd once thought handsome eased into a charming smile. "Is that any way to talk to a friend?"

"I'm not getting sucked into that conversation again, Tommy." She stopped five feet away from him. "And after that stunt you pulled with Brian, any sliver of sympathy I had for you is gone."

The smile faded and he tipped his head to one side, then sighed. "I've screwed this up."

"You've got one thing right, at least."

"And I'm sorry. I shouldn't have come on to you so strong about the money, but how was I to know that you'd gotten religion?"

"Wrong is wrong," she said. "My faith or lack of it has nothing to do with it."

He held out a beseeching glove-covered hand. "It's got everything to do with it, and you know it. I came here all those weeks ago thinking we were still friends—"

"We stopped being friends a long time ago." She took a steadying breath. "Tommy, just go."

At the same time he was saying, "You know Simon Graden would have had me killed if I hadn't testified against you."

"Well, he's dead now, and you're still messing around with all the same old stupid, illegal stuff." She made a shooing motion with her hand. "Same verse, same song. Go away, or I'm headed back inside to call the cops."

He scowled. "You owe me a favor, at least. Put in a good word with one of those rich friends of yours."

"No."

"I know about the company you're keeping these days, and I'm not just talking about your new boyfriend. I'm talking about those other people you know, like the ones you were hanging out with at that fancy party a couple of weeks ago."

"No." Her temper began to slip. "What part of no don't you understand?"

He moved away from her car. "Don't say I didn't give you an opportunity to be cooperative."

Without answering, she unlocked her car, started the engine and drove away without giving Tommy a backward glance. At the first traffic light, she took a steadying breath. She hadn't lost her temper, and she'd kept her vow to not engage in another circular discussion with him.

When she arrived home that evening a little past sundown, she realized that Christmas had arrived on her street when she hadn't paid attention. The older couple at the end of the block had tasteful white lights outlining the clean lines of their house. The family next door to Angela had the latest in huge blow-up figures, including a snowman whose top hat was taller than the eave of the house. Strings of blinking lights covered a spruce tree across the street. And she loved it all—the tacky and the tasteful—because it was a celebration of Christmas.

Still, when she opened the door to her home, she faced just how empty it—and her personal life—was. Not even a cat to welcome her home. She'd been so busy training dogs, she hadn't taken time to find one for herself.

Maybe if she had a dog, she wouldn't miss Brian quite as much. Being everywhere in the city now reminded her of him.

Her pep talk that she'd done the right thing echoed in her quiet home. As she went through her evening chores, everything failed to keep her attention. She finished decorating the small tree that she had put in front of the living room window. The task, though one she liked, served only to remind her that she was alone, much as she had always been. Usually she didn't mind it, but lately she found herself envying the companionship she'd witnessed with Rachel and Brian's families.

And there it was again. She just couldn't rid herself of the memory of the man she'd come to love. She missed his steadying presence.

She'd had a taste of what it was like to be with a man who was attentive and considerate. And she wanted more of that. A lot more, even though she'd done her best to slam the door between them.

Knowing she'd done the right thing didn't make it easier. Reverend Chester had always encouraged her to trust her faith and open her heart. Trusting her faith was easy, but opening her heart felt too much like following her heart's desire. And the truth was, she no longer trusted her heart to discern right from wrong. Logic told her she'd made the right decision to put some distance between herself and Brian. Her heart longed for his companionship with an intensity that felt too much like the cravings of addiction. And that proved to her she couldn't trust that feeling.

The daily updates with Maisey were a poor substitute for Brian's company, and she admitted she had the blues in a big way even though Jasper had passed the first battery of tests required for his certification. Next week, he'd have the final set, and just as promised, he'd be with Brian before Christmas.

When the ten o'clock news came on, she headed to the bedroom to change into her night clothes, her mind occupied with the two animal shelters she planned to visit the following day. Her focus changed, though, when she heard the announcer mention Brian's name.

Returning to the living room, she sank onto the couch and turned up the volume. The news anchor was saying, "A former Patriots quarterback is going blind. In a news conference this afternoon, Brian Ramsey put an end to the speculation that had surrounded his retirement last year. With his manager and his attorney at his side, he had this to say."

The imaged shifted to Brian. He looked wonderful to Angela, but tired, as well, as though the last few days had weighed as heavily on him as they had on her. His piercing eyes were on the camera. "My sight loss wouldn't be news except for two reasons. First, I had the privilege of playing football for most of my life, and I had the good fortune to do that professionally. Second—" he paused and took a breath before continuing "—as you know, rumors about my use of anabolic steroids have followed me for years. Unfortunately, they are true, which gets to the real point today. A combination of genetics, the injuries inherent to a contact sport like football and my use of an illegal substance all combined to leave me in the condition I am in today. I'm blind. And it was preventable." He paused again. "The other reason I chose to come forward with this today is to address the rumors that have circulated lately about the Beanstalk Gang and the work we do. We have a zero tolerance policy regarding illegal drugs. I formed this organization because I wanted kids to have access to the kinds of programs I did when I was a kid. As you know, most schools don't have the budgets for after-school programs like they used to. We fill that gap, and we want to continue to provide an environment where young people can participate in the things that interest them, whether it's sports or some other activity."

The picture on the television came back to the news anchor, who was asking a reporter what she made of the announcement. She expressed her opinion that no criminal investigation was likely since the abuse had happened years before. She expressed her belief that Brian seemed sincere and that the materials provided by his attorney after the news conference confirmed the medical diagnosis and the revelation that he'd soon be working with a guide dog named Jasper.

As the news moved on to other stories, Angela stared unfeelingly at the screen, proud of him and aching to call him. As she thought about his announcement more, she realized that his intent had been to defuse the accusations Andrew Brogg had made. She wished she believed it could work.

Unfortunately, she knew from experience that when

a reporter like Andrew was out to make a name for himself, he would be as tenacious as a bulldog after a bone. He wouldn't stop until he found his story. That made her afraid for herself and for Brian.

When there was a knock at her door the following morning, Brian was dead last on her list of people she expected to find on her stoop. But there he was, the collar of his down jacket turned up against the near zero temperature outside.

"Brian, what are you doing here?"

"I brought coffee," he said, holding a cardboard tray in front of him.

She looked beyond him and saw Sam sitting in the driver's seat of his car.

"Are you going to ask me in or simply stand here, letting all the heat out of your house?" Brian asked.

Smiling, she stood to the side, and when he didn't move, realized he hadn't seen that. "Come on in. Don't forget there's a step up." She waved to Sam, motioning him to come in, too, since it was cold outside. "You're out bright and early," she said, waiting at the door for Sam to come inside.

Sam grinned at her when he came through the door, carrying his own cup of coffee. "Great to see you," he said, casually touching her arm. He waggled his eyebrows in Brian's direction. "We've missed you."

Brian stood a couple of steps inside the room, the tray of coffee still in his hands. The smile on his face had turned from cheerful to determined.

"The coffee table is two steps in front of you," she told him.

He nodded, took the steps, and gingerly set down the coffee, then made his way to the sofa. His sight was gone, she realized. And her heart ached with the knowledge. They'd known this day was coming, and they had planned for it. Still, as she imagined the loss, she could sense how frustrated and scared he might be. Sensitive about it, too, since she didn't see the white cane.

"Jasper takes his final test at the end of the week," she said. "And Maisey tells me you're doing great."

"We are, and I can't wait until I get to take him home," Brian said. "But today, I'm here for you."

She didn't dare latch on to that—her dozens of reasons for wanting his company could only end in heartbreak.

Sitting down next to him, she picked up one of the coffees, and, seeing that it had cream in it, knew that it was the one intended for her. "Here you go," she said, handing him the other one. "How long has your sight been gone?"

The smile became more relaxed. "Leave it to you to cut to the chase." He brought the paper cup to his lips, finding the opening on the lid with a finger, and taking a sip. "It happened over the weekend. All that's left is a sliver of light. You know, like one of those late-afternoon streamers between a couple of slats in the blinds."

"Yes."

"It's irritating, to tell you the truth. I keep wanting to peek beyond the blind, and I can't."

Sam gave her a sympathetic look and took a seat on the rocker across the small room.

"Why are you here, Brian?" she repeated.

"I heard you were going dog hunting today, and I thought you might like some company."

Despite her resolve to stay away from him, her heart gave a little leap. Still... "I don't think that's a very good idea."

His smile faded and his sightless gaze turned inward. "That thing you said the other day about not wanting to see me agai—"

"I meant it, Brian. It's for the best."

"The best for you? Because I can sure tell you that it's not the best for me."

She felt her resolve wavering as her gaze slid to Sam. "You're coming, too?"

He shook his head while Brian said, "Sam's in college, you know. We're going to drop him by the library where he said he'd spend the day studying."

"Tired of riding in my car, huh?"

Brian grinned. "Well, if the only way I can talk you into putting up with my company is by folding myself up like an accordion into your little car, it's almost worth it."

She knew that if she let herself get talked into this, there'd be no room in her car for a new dog. The kennel took up the whole backseat and required that she bring the front seats as far forward as they would go. That made for a tight fit for herself, and it would be much worse for someone as tall as Brian.

As if reading her thoughts, he grinned and added, "Admit it. There's not room for me and a dog kennel in your car. And Maisey told me you always make new dogs ride in the kennel."

"She's right. I do."

His grin widened. "I suppose you could strap me to the roof."

The image of that made her laugh. Oh, how she had missed this. How she wanted it. Even if only for a day.

He took the folded white cane out of the inside pocket of his jacket and snapped it open. "Even strapped to the top of your little car, I could almost use this to find my way."

Once more she laughed, glad to see that his sense of humor about his situation remained intact.

Shaking her head at their silliness, Angela said, "I should warn you now, it's likely to be a boring day. I walk up and down the aisle looking at dogs and then looking at them again. And then, if I decide they have potential, I take them for a walk before giving them a battery of tests. You could be bored out of your mind."

"It won't happen," he assured her.

"Okay, okay. You can come, and we'll take your car. But I don't think making Sam wait around for us all day is right." She glanced at him. "You can use my car."

"That's nice of you. Thanks," Sam said. "But that's up to Brian."

"Fine with me," he said. "In fact, it's a good idea."

While she put on her coat, they decided that Sam would leave her car at Brian's house where he'd pick up his own, which left him free for the day.

After Sam left, she was alone with Brian and unaccountably uncomfortable, her words from the last time they'd been together echoing in her head. *I never want to see you again.* She'd both hated them and meant them.

"Maisey said you and Jasper are doing well," she said, mostly to fill up the silence.

"You said that already." He held out the car keys for her. "Don't make small talk, Angela. Not now. Not after everything we've been through."

"You're right."

She took a couple of steps forward to take the keys from him. He didn't drop them into her hand, however, but instead took hers. This close, she was too aware of him, too ready to lean her head against his chest and listen to his heart beat, too shaky for her own peace of mind.

"The deal with Andrew Brogg isn't going to be part of the dynamic between us," he said, his voice husky.

"There will always be someone like him, aiming to make a name for himself."

"Maybe, but you know as well as I do that you can't live your life worrying about what someone else might do."

"I don't want to cause problems for you," she whispered.

"I know. That was the main thing I kept thinking about the other night." He touched her cheek with the back of his fingers. "I found a really useful tool a couple of days ago—well, actually, Sam did. A braille version of the Bible that can be read from the computer and that allows you to search on specific words like, for instance, *faith*."

The change of topic surprised her, and she didn't know what to say.

"Want to know what I found out?" he asked.

"Yes."

"Faith is a pretty terrific thing."

She smiled. "I knew that."

"But did you know that it's to be sure of what you hope for and certain of what you do not see?"

"You've been reading." She watched him, taking in his smile and the warmth of his hand holding hers. He was on a path that included God, she realized. Just as she had prayed for.

His grin was infectious. "Listening is more like it, but yeah." He dropped the keys in her hand. "And, I'm beginning to understand a little bit about the source of your calm."

She chuckled. "I haven't been feeling very calm."

"You were entitled to a relapse." He clapped his hands together. "So, are you ready to go dog hunting?"

"I am." She led the way toward the door. "That sounds really horrible, you know. Like something you'd need a special season and a license for."

"Given the fate you're saving some of these dogs from, that isn't that far off."

When they reached the Escalade, she discovered that Sam had already put the dog crate in the back of the vehicle. And as she pulled away from the curb, she also noticed Andrew Brogg's too-familiar sedan a half block away. She didn't say anything to Brian, though. There was nothing they could do about Andrew, so no reason to bring it up.

They headed for the county animal shelter close to her house, arriving there a scant fifteen minutes later. As they got out of the vehicle, Angela once again noticed Andrew's car. Since the facility's parking lot was also the end of the street, he was stuck coming into the parking lot to turn around. She thought about confronting him, then decided if he wanted to have a boring day, following them from one shelter to another, he was welcome to it.

"Hey, Angela," called a woman as Brian and Angela came through the door.

The aroma of dogs and disinfectant hit him as he let Angela lead them across the room. He found himself listening to the way voices sounded, and he realized it was a large room without much to absorb the sound. He envisioned there was a concrete floor underneath them, and he suspected this was one of those large, all-purpose, metal warehouse-type buildings.

"How are you, Sandy?" Angela returned.

"Glad that you came. We have three dogs especially that I want you to look at." The woman laughed. "And then, you always pick one I didn't notice."

"Sandy, this is my friend, Brian Ramsey," Angela said, bringing their clasped hands forward enough that he felt a counter in front of them.

He appreciated the subtle gesture that helped him have a bearing on where he was in the room. He raised his right hand and discovered a tall counter.

"Nice to meet you," she said without a bit of recognition in her voice.

"You, too," Brian said, offering his hand.

She shook it, and he found himself analyzing that simple gesture, as well. Sandy wasn't very big, he decided, since her hand was small within his. Even smaller than Angela's slender one.

"Here are the pen numbers for the dogs I spotted," she said. "Just give Pete a yell when you're ready to look at any of them—he's back there somewhere."

"Will do."

Still holding his hand, she led the way toward a door, which she opened. The sound of barking dogs was immediately heard, and to Brian's ears, it wasn't a happy sound, but a distressed one. Dogs barking because they were upset, because they were scared, some simply because they had nothing else to do.

"Do you ever get used to the sound?" he asked, imagining what it must look like—longing faces with hopeful eyes watching through chain-link gates. He sensed the room was a large one, and he imagined rows of chain-link cages separated by aisles.

"It rips my heart out every single time," Angela said. "Do you have your cane with you?"

"Yep." It was folded and tucked away inside his jacket. He knew that he had to start using the thing, but he hated the public display that he was blind.

As if somehow understanding that, she said, "Now would be a good time to practice. Nobody is here but you and me."

He wanted to stare her down and had to laugh at himself about how futile that was. Despite his teasing her about it earlier, he hated the thing, hated that it marked him as different. Disabled. As always, the image of the blind beggar rose in his mind's eye, and as always, he pushed it away. Soon, he'd have Jasper…and another symbol that he was blind. He laughed.

"What?" she asked.

"I've been thinking that I didn't like the cane because it marks me as disabled. Like walking around with a guide dog won't."

"You're not the only person to feel that way."

"So be my eyes, Angela. What are we seeing and what are you looking for?"

"A dog that is no more than two years old, and a year or a bit more is even better. Sometimes you'll find a purebred here, like I found Jasper, but there are mostly mixed breeds. I'm looking for dogs whose parents were goldens, shepherds, Labs, boxers. And if I found another poodle, that would be something."

"You like my dog, huh?" Jasper wasn't staying with him at night yet, but he was counting down the days until he would.

"I love your dog," Angela replied. "I had a couple of great goldens that I trained about a year ago, and I didn't think I'd ever work with a dog that was more responsive than those two. Jasper is smarter than they were, and they really were stellar dogs."

Brian remembered his discomfort when he first met the dog, and he was also aware of just how much his perception had changed about that over the last week. He'd been able to see his dog before his sight was gone, thank God. The phrase echoed in his head, and he focused on it. Yeah. That was it exactly. Thank God, which must have been what his grandfather was getting at when they had first talked about the likelihood of him going blind. "You can moan about it, boy, with a 'why me?'. And you'll be miserable for the rest of your life. Or, you can be thankful for what you had and embrace that."

"Hello, pretty boy," Angela said, her voice bringing him back to the present. She must have bent over a little because her voice was lower to the floor than usual. "This guy is a boxer," she added. "His ears have been cropped, but it wasn't a very good job because they flop over at the top. He has a white blaze and a black mask, and there's just a touch of white on his chin and upper lip that makes him look like he's a candidate for a milk commercial."

Brian chuckled. "I relate to that."

"I bet you can," she said, then adding to the dog, "We'll be back to see you in a few minutes."

Brian knew she had moved away since he could hear her footfalls. Sweeping the cane in front of him as he'd been taught by the occupational therapist, he followed her. Once he stopped being self-conscious, it was easier.

Angela was focused on the dogs, telling him about the personality profile and obedience aptitude that she'd be doing with the couple of dogs she was interested in. She told Brian there were more than fifty dogs in the shelter, which explained the noise level. He learned the cages were as he had imagined as she explained how they were kept clean and how the dogs were fed and watered. Most of the dogs were males and most of them were forty to seventy pounds. The information tags on many of the cages indicated they had been surrendered rather than caught running at large as he had assumed.

They had been going up and down the aisles for more than a half hour when she gave a distressed sound. "There should be a special kind of torture for people who let this happen to a dog. This cocker spaniel is so matted that it will be hours shaving him down." The tone of her voice changed, and Brian knew that she'd once again knelt. "You don't deserve this, do you, boy." She stood, and her voice once again became brisk. "According to the information card, his owner brought him in, saying they were going on vacation and couldn't find anyone to watch the dog, so they were giving him up. Like he's an old pair of shoes or something. Can you believe it?"

"Do you ever think about adopting one of these dogs—just to have a dog?" he asked. "Not one to train for a service dog—just one to keep you company?"

"All the time. Especially when I see a guy like this who is as likely to be put down as he is to find a new home."

"So, why haven't you?"

"I don't know. I could say I'm busy, but that would be only partly right." She moved away from him. "I've lived alone for so long maybe I'm just scared to be responsible for someone else."

The admission stunned Brian.

It must have stunned her, too, because a couple of seconds later, she said, "Don't pay any attention to that. That's the Christmas blues talking, that's all."

Brian thought it was probably more than that. In fact, he was sure of it as he imagined her house the couple of times he'd been there. She lived simply, and that was to be expected since he doubted she had anything more than a modest income. But now that he thought about it, her tidy home was austere. He didn't remember seeing a single photograph or even a picture on the wall. It was as though she was still in some kind of prison, which maybe explained why she hadn't given herself the companionship of any other living thing.

She inspected the last of the kennels, then went to find Pete so she could further examine the two dogs she was interested in, the boxer and a golden retriever mix. Brian stayed behind, and he found his way back to the kennel holding the cocker spaniel, first to see if he could, but secondly drawn to the dog who had struck such a chord with Angela.

He couldn't get those two surprising things out of his head. That she was scared to be responsible for someone else when she was so responsible. And that she had the Christmas blues. He wondered if she had decorated her house for Christmas. He'd ask Sam about that later.

In front of the kennel, he knelt down on one knee and spoke softly to the dog. To his surprise, he heard the click of toenails against the cement and then felt the soft whoosh of the dog's breath against his fingers, the chain-link separating them.

"Looks like you have one of the qualities Angela said she liked," he told the dog. "You come to investigate. She's all business today, but I think she likes you."

At the sound of approaching footsteps, Brian lifted his head. One person, and not the familiar pattern of Angela's footfall's.

"Excuse me," Brian said, "can you tell me if the card has this dog's name on it?"

"Sure," returned a male voice, and a second later reading, "Ziggy. You interested in this dog?"

"I am," Brian said, thinking the voice sounded familiar. "What's the process to adopt?"

"Fill out the paperwork, I guess. Pay the fee." The man made a rude sound. "You're good at that. Paying. And then expecting others to pay, too."

"Do I know you?"

"Do you know me? Are you telling me that you can't see me?"

"No. I can't." Brian stood, holding his cane in front of him, trying to judge the distance between him and the man, more trying to place the voice.

"I heard you'd gone blind, but I didn't believe it. Everybody says it isn't true, white cane or not." The voice moved to his side, and a second later, the cane was kicked away and went clattering a few feet away. "You're not such a big man now, are you?"

"And you're proving you are?" Brian still didn't place the voice though it was familiar.

All of his senses were tuned in somehow in a way they hadn't been in months. Though the circumstances were completely different, he felt like he had in the middle of a big game when everything was on the line. He'd stand behind the center and look up and down the line, reading subtle changes in body language while he made the final adjustments in his own mind about how to finish the play. On the other side of the line were the players who wanted him intimidated, scared.

And after the snap, when things were going well, it was an incredible feeling of power, dropping into the pocket and knowing his pass would land the football exactly where he wanted it to. It had been like that all week when he'd sat on the bench in his dark closet and prayed. It was like that now, though he knew the intent was to have him scared.

And he recognized the voice. The kid he had believed in, who had assured him the police could have nothing on him because he hadn't done anything except hang out with his brother while he made a sale to an undercover cop. "What are you doing here, Ivan?"

FOURTEEN

"Just because you remembered my name—that don't mean nothing," Ivan said, sounding more like the teenager that he was, angry and sullen today.

Brian remembered being an angry teenager himself, and admitted that was part of what had drawn him to Ivan. Arguing with his logic wouldn't get them anywhere.

"This is a little off the beaten path for you. How did you know I'd be here?" As he asked the question, he was also listening for Angela.

"I know stuff."

No doubt about that, Brian thought. "That doesn't answer the question."

Brian could hear the kid shift from one foot to another, and he wished that he could see Ivan's expression.

"I was surprised to see you, but you didn't seem surprised to see me."

"You can't see nothing," Ivan said. "And I knew you were going to be here."

How, Brian wondered, ignoring the taunt. "So you found me. What's on your mind?"

"I...uh..."

Stranger and stranger, Brian thought, comparing this conversation to one they'd had in his office the week before Thanksgiving. Then, Ivan had been sure of himself, polite, and he had made a convincing argument to have a second chance at the Beanstalk Gang, saying the activities, especially basketball, provided sanity in his life.

As Brian faced the young man, he imagined what he'd say to him if he could simply see. Despite the fact that Ivan had kicked away his cane, if he had intended any real harm he would have tried it by now.

"If I remember right, you don't have wheels," Brian said. "How did you get here?"

"A friend."

Brian took a step forward, and when he heard Ivan back up a step, he inwardly smiled. The kid definitely wasn't as cocky as he'd initially come off.

"The same friend who told you I was here?" One more step forward.

Ivan backed up again. "No."

"What's your friend's name?" When Brian stepped forward this time, he felt the cane beneath his feet, and he bent to pick it up.

"How'd you do that? I mean, if you can't see and all."

"Sight is only one of the senses. You were going to tell me your friend's name, and then you were going to tell me what you're doing here." Brian made sure his voice sounded authoritative.

"You owe me," Ivan said, the words sounding forced, as though he'd just then remembered what he was going to say.

Brian took a step in the direction of his voice. "I doubt that, but just for the sake of conversation, exactly what do I owe you?" And he kept wondering where Angela was. Ivan's older brother was trouble, and if he was the one who had driven the kid out here...

"I'm tired of you butting into my life."

"I see." Brian scratched his head, pretending to think. "You're the same guy who lives to be on Coach Norris's basketball team. And the one who hangs around the office because you've got a crush on Jodie. And the one who told me that you were in my debt after I bailed you out of jail when you were stupid enough to tag after your brother when he was dealing to an undercover cop. Is that right?"

"Well....maybe I don't want to play anymore." He sounded uncertain, and the more he talked the more Brian was convinced that someone else had tried to fill his head with ideas—ideas that weren't sticking very well.

"That's easy. Just quit."

"I'm no quitter," Ivan said, the first real conviction in his voice since he'd shown up.

"Who brought you here?" Brian asked.

"A guy named Tommy Man—"

"Tommy Manderoll?" *Him* again. "Did he come inside with you?" Brian cocked his head to the side, listening. All he heard were the dogs barking, a sound that had somehow faded to the background during the few minutes he and Ivan had been talking. A door on the opposite side of the large room opened and closed, and then he heard the murmur of Angela's voice. She didn't sound upset, so whomever she was talking to couldn't be Tommy.

"Brian," she called. "Where are you?"

"Over here by the cocker spaniel," he returned.

A second later, he heard her footsteps coming up behind Ivan. "It took me a minute to find Pete. He's getting out the two dogs I'm interested in." She stopped talking when she reached them. "Hello," she said to Ivan.

"Hey," he said, then tacked on a second later, "This your woman?"

"This is Angela London," Brian said. "She trained my guide dog." He waved in Ivan's direction. "This is Ivan Fletcher."

"Nice to meet you," she said. "Ah, here comes Pete. Even though it's cold outside, I'm taking them out to the yard."

"I'll catch up in a minute," Brian said.

"Are you sure?"

He nodded. After he heard her and Pete move away with the dogs, he said to Ivan, "Let's go see your new friend."

"I don't think that's a good idea, man."

"It's what we're going to do anyway. Let's go." Brian stepped briskly forward, sweeping the cane in front of him, each tap subtly marking the next place he'd place his foot, determined that Ivan would have no idea that he felt naked and exposed as a newborn baby. They reached the door to the lobby, and Brian waited for Ivan to catch up and open it.

"Sandy," he called, striding toward the counter and hoping he'd correctly remembered her name.

"Yes?" she answered.

"I have a favor to ask."

"If I can," she said.

He smiled. "I'm going outside with this young man, and if I'm not back in here in two minutes, call the cops."

She didn't reply.

"Sandy?"

"Yeah. Sure. Two minutes. Call the cops."

"You've got it."

He waved toward Ivan. "Let's go."

"This wasn't my idea," Ivan grumbled as they went outside, the cold air biting.

"I already figured that out." Sensing that Ivan was close enough to touch, Brian reached for him, taking his arm just above the elbow. "I want you to go to the driver's side of the car."

"Okay."

The easy agreement surprised Brian. "Anyone with you besides Tommy?"

"No."

"And just so I'm clear, how did you know we were here? Was Tommy following us?" If he was it was long past time to get a restraining order.

"No, man. We were just hanging out, and some dude called on the cell phone about an hour ago, and we came here."

So someone else had followed them.

Ivan came to a stop at the driver's side of a vehicle, and Brian tapped on the window.

The window didn't come down.

"What's he doing?" Brian asked.

"He's mouthing that he doesn't want to talk to you."

"Sure you do." Brian raised his voice and knocked on the window again. "You didn't make friends with Ivan and come all the way out here to sit in your car like a coward."

Brian heard the click of a lock, and he stepped back.

"This guy have any bruises on his face?" Brian asked Ivan.

"A couple."

"I figured you'd stay hidden behind Angela's skirts," Tommy said, getting out of the car.

"You figured wrong," Brian said. "Now instead of sending Ivan in to do your dirty work, why don't you tell me what this whole cloak-and-dagger bit is about."

"I think you already know."

"I don't play games. Spill it or leave."

"Kid, why don't you get in the car," Tommy said.

"See ya," Ivan said.

"Afraid to be overheard," Brian said after he heard Ivan get into the car.

"I thought you'd like to know I've been recruiting. Starting with your friend Ivan. And you might have noticed. He's not the sharpest pencil in the box—"

"Must be the company he's been keeping lately."

"But he's useful," Tommy said. "I know just how much having this poster boy means to you. So here's the deal. Invest a half million in my enterprise, and I'll make sure I've got Ivan's back covered."

Brian stared in the direction of Tommy's voice. "You want money?"

"You owe me," Tommy said, the inflection sounding so much like what Ivan had said minutes earlier. "Invest, and I won't recruit from your organization. Invest, and you can pretend to have the squeaky-clean operation you want everyone to think you have."

Brian shook his head. "You're barking up the wrong tree, pal. And you're as stupid as you've accused Ivan of being if you think that, one, I'm going to give you a penny, and two, that I won't call the cops down on you."

"You've been warned."

"Ditto," Brian returned. When he heard the car door open, he added, "Ivan, if you want a ride home, I'll see that you get it."

There was a moment of silence while he imagined the silent exchange between Tommy and Ivan. Finally, Ivan said, "I'm good."

The car's engine started, and Brian stepped back, feeling his heel collide with the curb. He stepped onto the sidewalk and realized he'd made an error in not paying attention to how many steps it was before the turn to the front door.

He listened to Tommy's car driving away while he headed back toward the front door, sweeping his cane in front of him. To his relief, he felt where the sidewalk turned, and he realized the air in front of him felt somehow different, as though the mass of the building loomed close. A second later, his cane touched the edge of the building, and he slowed. Sure enough, the door was right in front of him. He opened it and stepped inside.

"That was two and a half minutes," Sandy said from

his right, evidently looking out the window. "Everything all right?"

"Fine," he said, now wondering if Andrew Brogg was the missing piece of this puzzle. "Are there any other cars out there? Especially a beige or gray sedan being driven by a guy wearing glasses?"

"Don't see a soul," she said.

Just because he wasn't there now didn't mean that he hadn't followed them here. But that was something he'd never be able to prove. "Which way to the yard?" he asked Sandy. "I want to go watch Angela in action."

His statement echoed in his head, along with the hundred other things that were part of ordinary conversation. Seeing, looking, watching...and to use other words was awkward in the extreme. Sensing Sandy beside him, he turned his head, half expecting the dark void to dissipate so he could see her.

"But before we do that, there's a cocker spaniel in the back that I want to know about."

"There are a couple," Sandy said. "Do you remember which one?"

"Angela said this one was extremely matted. Something about his owners going on vacation."

"Ah, I remember that one. An older man brought him in. This poor dog hasn't had a bath or a bit of attention and he said the dog was too much for them."

"That sounds like the one," Brian said. "I'd like to adopt him, but I can't take him until tomorrow."

She touched his arm. "That's wonderful. He's a sweetheart, but in such a mess that nobody seemed interested. Let me pull his file."

She walked away, and Brian followed her back across the room, really paying attention to the feedback the cane was providing to him about the space. He could do this, he thought. He'd confronted Ivan and that creep, Tommy, and that had turned out okay. As different coaches had told him dozens of times over the years, act like you know what you are doing until you do.

A moment later, Sandy made a sound of distress. "This dog tested positive for heartworm."

"Meds take care of that, right?"

"Most of the time," she replied, going on to tell him about the possible risks and adding that he'd be facing a big grooming bill on top of whatever the cost would be to take care of the heartworms.

"You're not talking me out of this," Brian told her. "The dog caught Angela's eye, and that's enough of a recommendation to know he should get another chance."

"Okay, then. Let's get started with the paperwork."

Fifteen minutes later, it was all finished, and Sandy guided him toward the yard where Angela was evaluating the two dogs.

"I was beginning to think you'd gotten lost," Angela said as he made his way down a pebble-covered walk toward her.

"Nope. How are the dogs?"

"The boxer has potential. The other one I'm not so sure about. He'd make a wonderful pet for someone but his attention isn't as focused as I'd like it to be."

"Maybe he's nervous. You know, test anxiety."

She laughed. "I remember having that myself."

Over the next half hour, Brian listened to Angela put

one dog then the other through an evaluation that tested whether they already knew basic commands, how readily they paid attention to her. She eventually decided the boxer was the only dog she'd take. Listening to her praise about how smart the dog was, Brian began to wonder if his idea of adopting the cocker spaniel and giving it to her was such a good idea. If it turned out not to be, he figured his house was big enough for two dogs.

She filled out the paperwork for the dog and paid the fee to adopt him. Angela laughed when they headed for Brian's vehicle because the dog's demeanor completely changed the instant they headed for the parking lot.

"I wish you could see him," she said to Brian after they were settled into the car and had pulled out of the parking lot. "He's a happy boy, though the next stop is the vet's office, and so that may have him worried again. He'll need to stay there a couple of days, get a checkup and make sure he doesn't have anything contagious that could be spread to the other dogs at Guardian Paws."

"And then training begins," he said.

"It does. And hopefully, he'll live up to his potential. If he doesn't, he'll end up being someone's very well-trained pet."

Brian thought about all the animals they'd seen today, and she'd tested only two, then rescued only one. "So, it's not automatic that he'll become a service dog?"

"No. Of the dogs we rescue, only about one in five goes on to become a service dog."

"I had no idea."

"The ones that break my heart are the old guys who

are no longer cared for because someone got bored or they got old or who knows why."

"Like the cocker spaniel?"

"Like the cocker spaniel," she agreed. "I can't get him out of my mind."

The worry in Brian's chest eased at that, and he trusted his hunch that he'd done the right thing. Tomorrow he and Sam would come back for the dog, and thanks to listening to Angela's process, knew that both a groomer and a veterinarian were on his list of people to find.

By the time they had taken the boxer to the vet's office and left the dog for its evaluation, it was past lunchtime. Before they headed to the next shelter, Brian talked Angela into stopping for a bite. She didn't want to take time for a sit-down lunch, so they ordered a submarine sandwich to share, then ate it in the car in the parking lot of the next shelter on their list.

The conversation flowed easily between them while they ate, and Brian decided he was glad that she hadn't wanted to go to a café. Here, there were no outside distractions, and he could simply focus on what she was saying and imagine how she looked. She'd always worn one of two coats when they'd been out, one a deep burgundy that made her skin look like ivory velvet. The other was a midnight blue, and he'd always liked how it made her eyes look, enhancing gray or blue specks within the depths of the iris that he didn't see at other times. He liked the positive way that she looked at everything, which he still didn't understand. With her past and her prison record, she had reason to be harder than she was. Firm as she was with the dogs, the only time he'd seen that hardness was when she'd confronted Tommy. Given his own experiences with that, he now understood.

Brian supposed he should tell her about that, and he was thinking about that when she said, "I've been arguing with myself all morning on whether to tell you that I saw Andrew Brogg this morning." She was silent a moment, then added, "He followed us to the shelter. Talk about someone who keeps turning up like mold on bread."

"Then I suppose this would be a good time to tell you that Tommy Manderoll was also there."

"He was?"

"He's the one who brought Ivan out there, and he made it pretty clear that I can invest—as he calls it— or he'll turn Ivan into a mule."

At once there was the soft touch of Angela's hand over his. "Oh, Brian. I'm so sorry."

"It's a stupid plan he has, and it won't work."

"But thanks to me, you've got this to deal with on top of everything else."

Brian turned his hand so he was clasping hers. "The way I figure it is that it all works out okay. Thanks to you, I found my path through faith again. I have a terrific dog that will be living with me by the end of the week—"

"If he passes his last test."

"He'll pass, I'm sure of it." Brian squeezed her hand. "And I got to know you. Tommy is a small price to pay for that."

Angela felt an enormous lump form in her throat at Brian's declaration. She studied his face, and his brilliant eyes were so intent on her that she had to remind herself that he wasn't seeing her. The connection she felt with him, though, was just as deep as it would have been had their gazes been locked.

Oh, how I love him, she thought.

She turned her head and stared outside at the winter day, which was one of those beautiful, perfect, Colorado days with a blue sky and enough snow on the ground to put a person in the Christmas spirit. She longed to think that what they had between them could be this perfect. But it wouldn't be. Even if Tommy's plan was as stupid as Brian believed, there was still Andrew Brogg. And if it wasn't Andrew, it would be someone else.

A tear slipped from the corner of her eye. She looked up, and, sitting across the parking lot from them not twenty feet away, watching like he always was, was Andrew Brogg in his car.

When her gaze met his, he smirked and gave her a salute.

With awful clarity, she knew as surely as she was sitting here that Andrew had called Tommy. Remembering what he'd said to her just yesterday—*you will help, you just don't know it yet*—she knew that Andrew was pulling some strings with Tommy who in turn was manipulating Ivan. And she finally recognized the expression she'd seen in Tommy's eyes yesterday.

Bone-deep fear.

FIFTEEN

"Andrew Brogg is here again, still watching," Angela said after a moment.

Brian crumpled the paper that had wrapped his sandwich into a tight ball. "Unfortunately, there's not much we can do about that."

"That is the awful part," she agreed.

"I am going to talk to my attorney after I get home," Brian added. "Between Brogg and Manderoll, I've had enough. What Brogg is doing may be legal, but it has to come under the heading of harassment, don't you think?" Without waiting for an answer, he added, "And as for Manderoll, shaking me down for money and threatening to use kids from my organization to form a drug network, if that's not illegal, I want to know why."

"He's desperate," Angela said. "And desperate people do stupid, sometimes terrible things. Trust me, I know."

"Hey." Brian reached toward her, his hand unerringly finding hers. "I shouldn't have gone off like that. Unfortunately, we can't do anything about either of these guys at the moment. So…time to think about happier things, don't you think?"

With that, they headed inside. Unlike the county shelter where they'd been earlier, this place was busy, especially for a weekday. Seeing that always pleased Angela since it meant that a lot of dogs and cats would be getting a well-deserved second chance.

This time, she didn't find any dogs that she wanted to adopt, though the three she brought out for evaluation were nice animals that would make someone wonderful pets.

When they came out of the shelter an hour and a half later, Andrew was gone. He wasn't out of mind, though, as she headed toward Brian's house. They arrived there more than an hour later after navigating through rush-hour traffic. Her car was parked next to the garage. As she hit the button to open the garage door and parked Brian's car inside, she admitted to herself that she wasn't quite ready for the day to end even though it had to.

"Would you like to go for a walk and look at the Christmas lights in the neighborhood before you go?" he asked. "They're spectacular."

Taking the key out of the ignition, she looked over at him. "How would you know that?"

He grinned. "Nonnie keeps telling me. And I remember from last Christmas. If they're like that, she's right."

When Angela didn't answer right away, he got out of the car and came around to the driver's side, opening the door and holding out his hand. As if sensing her conflicting thoughts he said, "Like I told you this morning, I don't want Brogg or anyone else to be part of the dynamic between you and me."

She cupped his cheek with her hand, his skin smooth and warm beneath her palm. "How can he not be? He's out there, planning his next move—"

"No doubt. But are you going to let this guy define who you are? I'm wishing right now that I'd been a student of the Bible for a long time and I could give you some meaningful quote that would illustrate what I know right here." He touched the center of his chest. "But that's not me. What I know is football strategy. There are times when you see the opportunity to go for the big play and the seventy-five-yard touchdown play. But most of the time, it's a matter of getting down the field five yards at a time, one down at a time, until the goal is in sight."

"Every man shall receive his reward according to his own labor," she said. "Corinthians, I think."

He smiled. "See? I knew there was a verse."

"Probably more than one."

"The point is, of course, he has a plan. But we can't decide what to do based on that. We have to go with our own values and our own strengths. Weren't you the one who told me that you just have to keep moving forward in faith as though your prayers are at work?"

She could have sworn that she remembered in detail every exchange between them, but she didn't remember this. "That sounds like something I would have said."

"It's good advice."

Juxtaposed to everything Brian stood for and was trying to accomplish with his foundation was the harm that Andrew could do through the court of public opinion. Since she'd been on the receiving end of a reporter's innuendo and self-serving interpretation of the facts, she knew too well what could happen. Her old reputation and her prison record could be skewed, used against Brian. No way did she want that to happen.

The door to the house opened, and Olivia stood there. "I thought I heard your car," she said. "Your grandfather sent me to see if there's anything you need."

"Make sure I'm all right is more like it," Brian returned, his voice teasing. "We'll be right in."

"It's great to see you, Angela. After Sam delivered your car, we set another place for dinner."

"I—"

"Don't say it," Brian said to her, leaning close, then closer still, until his cheek grazed hers. "Stay. Please."

Closing her eyes, she savored the contact. *Help me do what's right* was her automatic, silent prayer.

"This time of year Nonnie loves playing Christmas carols. When was the last time you stood around a piano and sang like that?"

"I don't think I ever have," she admitted.

"That settles it, then." He leaned closer, his lips skimming across her cheek.

"You're very persuasive," she grumbled, her heart not in the complaint at all.

"I know," he admitted without any conceit.

The meal was just as wonderful as she had remembered from last time. As Angela watched the exchanges between Brian and his grandfather, she had the feeling something had shifted in their relationship—it didn't seem as strained as it had last time. And, boy, was the house decked out in holiday color. A tall fir decorated in white lights and sparkling clear glass ornaments dominated the window in the living room. The thing Angela liked best about all the decorations, though, was Nonnie's collection of Nativity scenes. Large ones that looked as though they had emerged from a Renaissance painting, brass ones, ceramic ones and the one she liked the best—a small, plain set made out of olive wood.

And, as Brian had promised, they gathered around the piano after dinner, listening to Nonnie play and singing carols. Angela absorbed it all, knowing this would stand out as one of the most special times of her life. She would forever remember the sight and sound of Brian and Gramps leaning against the piano, their baritone voices soaring with the sound of "Silent Night," the sound of it bringing tears to her eyes. When the song faded, she noticed that Olivia also had tears in her eyes.

And when they were finished, Brian insisted they go for the walk to see the Christmas lights. Gramps and Nonnie begged off.

"You know what my real intent was," Brian said after they were outside and strolling down the driveway toward the street.

"What?"

His hand tightened around hers. "To walk like this with you. If Jasper was with us, we'd be hitting a fast pace. Since he's not, we have to walk shoulder-to-shoulder."

"Have to, hmm?" she teased.

"Unless you think I ought to be practicing with my cane."

"You had a lot of that today," she said.

"The Jacksons live next door," he said, "and last year they set up a forest of stylized Christmas trees in the front yard."

She looked away from Brian to the yard in question. "They did this year, too."

"And the Evans family is across the street. I can hear the blower, so they must have the big plastic ornaments up."

"A Santa inside a big snow globe," she confirmed. "Do you really want to talk about all your neighbors' decorations?"

He shook his head. "No. I just want to walk with you." They walked only a few feet before he added, "Did you know that when you left me in the shelter today that it was the first time I'd been alone outside the house since I lost my sight?"

"Really?"

"Yep. At first, it was a little strange because I hadn't paid that close attention to where we were as we went up and down the aisle, but then I wanted to see if I could find my way back to Ziggy—"

"Who?"

"That cocker spaniel. His name is Ziggy. Anyway, I did, and I was feeling pretty smug."

"That's not necessarily a bad thing."

"No. But the whole thing was a reminder that whether I like it or not, things have changed now." He stopped walking and turned toward her. "Which coat are you wearing—the burgundy one or the blue one?"

"The blue one," she said. "It's warmer. Why?"

"I'm just imagining how you look." With his free

hand, he touched the side of her face, his fingers cold. "Your hair is down today?"

"Yes," she whispered, her voice suddenly choking up. "My ears would be freezing otherwise."

"I have a pair of earmuffs if you want to borrow them."

"I'm okay."

"I'm not," he said, his voice soft, husky. "You don't know how much I've missed you these last two weeks."

She didn't dare tell him that she had missed him, as well.

"Any chance you'll change your mind and finish up this last week of training with me?"

His voice sounded so hopeful, and to this moment the evening had been so lovely that she longed to give him what he wanted. He deserved so much more than the simple "no" that she had to say. And she wasn't at all sure she could make him understand.

Ahead of them another brilliant yard with its holiday display loomed, the twinkling lights shimmering in the night like possibility and hope.

More time had elapsed than she had intended, she realized, when Brian turned them around to head back to his house. "Your silence says it all."

"Wait." She pulled on his arm, bringing them once more to a stop. "Do you have any idea how much I want to simply say yes and follow my heart?"

"Then do it," he gruffly said.

"I don't trust my heart. I don't."

He looked at her, and she had to remind herself that

he didn't see her, couldn't read the anguish in her expression that surely matched what was inside.

She searched for the words that would somehow help him understand. "When I make choices out of my own wants, I'm never, ever certain I've made the right one. In fact, I've made terrible choices in the name of doing what I wanted, and others have paid a huge price for it—"

"Your friend Rachel."

"Yes. Yes."

"You're too hard on yourself," Brian said.

Facing him, she took off both her gloves, then pressed her palms against his cheeks. He took a ragged breath and placed both of his gloved hands over hers.

"When I followed my heart and did what I wanted," she said, "I ruined my best friend. The faith that I found in prison keeps me from making the same mistake again. I won't do that to you. I won't."

"This isn't the same."

"It is to me." She stood on tiptoe and kissed him, intending it to be a quick goodbye. But then he wrapped his arms around her and drew her close. Lowering his head, he kissed her again, as thoroughly and sweetly as she ever had been. She clung to him, her heart cracking open because she knew this would be her only moment in his arms.

Hot tears slipped from beneath her closed eyes, instantly cold as they slid between the icy night air and her warmer cheeks.

Within his arms, Brian felt her shudder, knew that she was trying hard not to sob. He understood that since he wanted to howl at the moon in his own pain. He sensed there was no changing her mind, which at once made him admire her for her convictions and despair for the two of them over this lost potential to have a life together.

At last he understood her. She didn't think she was deserving of God's forgiveness, and she was doing penance for the wrongs she'd done in her past, a penance that might never end for her since she didn't trust her own judgment about herself.

They walked arm in arm back to the house in silence. Brian didn't know what to say to her, and she seemed lost in her own thoughts. Her posture was rigid as though she was holding herself together by sheer will.

He listened to the cheerfulness in her voice as she bade Nonnie and Gramps good-night and wished them a Merry Christmas. He wondered if anyone heard just how forced it was. Following her to her car, he said, "Call me when you get home, just so I know you made it okay."

"I can't," she softly replied. "You're just going to have to trust that no news is good news."

And with that, she was gone.

SIXTEEN

When Angela got home that evening she was greeted by silence. Not even a goldfish to greet her. That morose thought sparked a long-ago memory of her Christmas request of her dad the first year after her mother had died. Angela had become a latchkey child, locking herself in the house as her father had instructed when she got home from school. She'd never been more lonely, and she had asked for a dog for Christmas. On Christmas morning, a small stuffed one had been left under the tree instead of the live companion she had hoped for.

Now she hung up her coat and looked around at her spare furnishings and the small Christmas tree that she had set up in front of the living room window a few days ago.

She plugged in the lights on the tree and burst into tears.

Reverend Chester had told her dozens of times that God had forgiven her, and she believed him. But how could she forgive herself? How could she trust her own judgment that following her heart's desire wouldn't once more hurt the people she loved? This bone-deep ache for Brian's company felt too much like the one that had led her to experiment with drugs and into the disastrous relationship with Tommy.

She had made a vow to herself that she would never again bring the kind of harm to another person that she'd brought to Rachel and her children. And that meant staying away from Brian. That meant somehow getting a step ahead of Andrew Brogg, if her suspicions were correct that he was manipulating Tommy. Only she had no idea how.

Drying her tears and squaring her shoulders, she went to the kitchen and found it as tidy as it had been this morning when she'd left with Brian—a lifetime ago, it seemed. Seeing the light flashing on the phone answering machine, she pushed the playback button. The first message was from Tommy, another of his desperate-sounding "we've got to talk" demands, which she erased. The second was from Micah McLeod. After checking that it wasn't too late to call, she dialed his number.

"Tommy is in way over his head this time," Micah told her after they'd said their hellos. "He's gotten himself mixed up with a dangerous cartel. I can't tell you much more than that because it's an ongoing investigation, but I wanted to warn you to stay alert. And call me if there's anything—and I mean anything—that you need."

"Thanks for the heads-up," she said, then added. "I think he must owe them money or something." She related Tommy's confrontation with Brian, ending with, "He's never been so stupid as to make threats before."

"I think your assessment is dead-on," Micah said. "He's desperate, which makes him dangerous. And as for his recruiting—we can do something about that. Have your friend call me."

After she hung up, she dialed Brian's cell phone number, praying she'd be able to just leave him a message since she didn't know what she'd say to him after telling him that she wouldn't call him. Instead, he answered.

"You okay?" he immediately said.

"Fine," she answered, her heart giving a little leap at the sound of his voice and at his concern for her.

"I just wondered, since you'd said you wouldn't call."

"I'm fine," she repeated, then passed along Micah's message and his telephone number. She wanted to add more—that she was sorry for hurting him, sorry that she had kissed him—only she wasn't. Sorry she wouldn't be there when he got to take Jasper home. Tears burned in her eyes when she realized he'd be getting a dog for Christmas. He deserved it, and she was happy for him despite wanting the same for herself.

"This is good," Brian was saying. "Thanks."

"You're welcome." She closed her eyes, and while she still had the courage to walk away from him, whispered, "Good night."

Brian held the phone to his ear for several seconds after it went dead. He'd wanted to tell her this was among the dozens of things she was doing that proved she was a different person than the one she had described herself as being before. He just didn't know how to make her believe it.

The following morning, Sam picked him up shortly

before eight for what promised to be a very busy day. Brian's list was long. Adopt Ziggy, the cocker spaniel. See his attorney. Meet with Special Agent McLeod. Train with Jasper. Take Ziggy to the vet and to the groomer. Buy supplies for Ziggy. Meet with staff at the Beanstalk Gang.

Despite the long list, Angela was at the center of his thoughts. "How do you help someone let go of the past?"

He didn't realize he'd even said the words aloud until Sam said, "You mean like Scrooge and the clanking chains of Christmas past?"

Brian chuckled. "Exactly."

"Prayer," Sam instantly said, the way he always did when he thought practicing faith was the answer.

And, at last, Brian was beginning to understand why Sam believed as he did. This issue with Angela wasn't one that he could power his way through. Instead, he'd have to follow the path that God showed him. Letting go of control to do that was a scary thing, Brian admitted to himself.

Help me see the answers, he silently prayed. *Help Angela to understand that she's worthy of forgiveness— and love.*

Their first stop was Gil York's office. During the night, Brian had decided that the first step toward making Angela believe that she wasn't hurting him, could never hurt him, was to deal with Andrew Brogg. Brian explained the situation to his attorney as succinctly as he could.

"Has he gotten out of his car and talked to you?" Gil

asked. "Overtly threatened you—I mean physically, not just writing a story about you?"

"Nope. Just followed us, which he's been doing for weeks now, at least a couple of times a week."

"I don't see how we can take any action against him," Gil said. "Even if he's called other people like you've said, unless they've committed some crime, having him follow you around isn't illegal. And if there's a connection between him and the television report the other night, I haven't found it."

"Yet," Brian added.

"Maybe not at all. We can't rule out other sources. I haven't been able to get through the prison red tape yet to speak with your former dealer but I'm working on it. We have to consider that he is the source for the story the other night."

"So we're stuck with Brogg being my shadow?"

"For the moment."

Brian left the office feeling the kind of frustration he'd had when things began going sour in a big game. Adjustments had to be made in the offense, and soon. Too much was at stake—the reputation of the Beanstalk Gang and their plans to expand the programs they offered. And more importantly, the future that he wanted for Angela that wouldn't—couldn't—happen until she believed the threat of Brogg and people like him was removed.

Fortunately, the meeting with Micah McLeod went better. Brian gathered that the man had been involved with Angela's arrest, and to his surprise, she seemed to bear him no ill will at all. He appeared to have an equal respect for Angela.

Micah and Brian discussed the best way to deal with the threat that Tommy represented directly and the other temptations in the neighborhood. After some brainstorming, they decided a *Survivor*-type camp that exposed the kids to some high adventure and the type of training DEA agents went through would be a good way to educate the kids and at the same time provide a deterrent.

Brian liked the man, but he still didn't understand why his interest in Angela was this personal. As Micah was getting ready to leave, Brian said, "I don't quite get why you're so willing to go out of your way for Angela."

Micah took a moment to answer. "I owe Angela a lot. If it weren't for her, Rachel and I would have never gotten together."

Rachel, the childhood friend that she'd been in business with. If Angela had mentioned she was married to the DEA agent, Brian didn't remember.

"She's family," Micah added, "though generally she has a hard time believing that. And you know how it is with family—sometimes there's a rough patch that has to be worked out."

Brian understood, since he'd been there with his grandfather more times that he cared to remember. He was glad to know that Angela had family, or at least people who viewed her as such. If things between the two of them didn't work out as he wanted, at least she wouldn't be as alone as he had once feared she was.

The next stop was the animal shelter, where Brian finished the process to adopt the cocker spaniel.

"This is the mangiest dog I've ever seen," Sam said when they came out of the facility with the dog on his brand-new leash. "Your car is going to need detailing after having this guy in it."

"Maybe. But it will be better after he's groomed."

They dropped the dog by the vet's office, where the dog endured his checkup like a rookie waiting to be told he'd have to do laps after screwing up. From there, they went to the groomer, then Brian and Sam headed to Guardian Paws for training with Jasper.

After they were finished with that, Brian realized he'd committed to bring a dog home on a night when he was the only one in the house—his grandparents were going to a holiday party. The dozens of things that could go wrong began to weigh on him.

He spent the afternoon at the Beanstalk Gang office while Sam went to class. Just before Sam was due to arrive to take him to pick up Ziggy, his cell phone rang. The groomer was on the other end of the line saying she wouldn't be able to finish the dog before the end of the day, and she wanted permission to take him home.

"Fine," Brian told her, as they agreed on the time when he could pick up the dog the following day.

That evening, Brian and Sam arrived home to an empty house. Though it had been an extremely busy day, Angela had never been far from Brian's thoughts. Now that they were back at the house and putting away the supplies they had purchased for the cocker spaniel, she was front and center once more. He'd imagined a dozen different scenarios for giving her the dog, and he'd dismissed every single one as too cheesy or sentimental or stupid.

"You going to hand me that sack of toys," Sam asked, bringing Brian's attention back to the moment, "or leave me to do all the work myself?"

"Nag, nag, nag." Brian handed Sam the bag he had retrieved from the back of the car.

"This dog is going to have more toys than a kid on Christmas morning," Sam said, carrying the bag to the spot in the garage where they had decided to stack everything. In addition to toys, there was a kennel, a separate bed, food, brushes and a leash. "You know, we're just going to have to load all this stuff up again in a day or two."

"I know." Brian reached inside once more, this time finding the bed and dragging it toward the door. "But, I don't want to leave it in the car."

They finished putting things away, and then Sam left for the evening.

As Brian settled in, the house seemed to echo as he moved through it. Using the techniques taught to him by the occupational therapist, he got the dinner that had been left for him out of the refrigerator and put it in the microwave oven. He turned on the television and listened with half an ear as he ate. Without a picture, the dialogue sounded stupid, and he turned it off. In the silence, he imagined the house filled with a family that included more than his grandparents. A wife. Children. For a while, those dreams had seemed dead after Erica had decided to break off their engagement. Now that he knew Angela, he couldn't remember why Erica had seemed so appealing.

When the telephone rang an hour later, it was a relief to have the interruption.

"Brian, this is Ivan Fletcher" came the kid's anxious-sounding voice over the phone.

Brian was surprised the kid had his home telephone number since it was unlisted. "What's up, kid?"

"I don't know who else to call," Ivan said. "I've been with Tommy all day, and he's been talking crazy, man. He called some dude, and they had a big, long argument, and when it was done, he started saying everything was Angela's fault. Over and over. It's all Angela's fault. And we were driving there, and I kept telling him, hey, man, you can't go there, let's just think about this and wait a while. He got mad at me and kicked me out of the car."

Everything stopped for an instant, frozen in time like some horrible snapshot while Brian's mind raced. He knew that Ivan would have no reason to tell him if it weren't so. Unless this was more of yesterday's nonsense when Ivan had confronted him.

"You promise this is on the up-and-up, Ivan?"

"I'm not lying."

"Okay, then." Brian disconnected the call and was in the process of dialing 911 when he decided he'd better call Angela first. If she was there, she could leave the house, and everything would be okay. He pressed the speed dial for her number on his cell phone, and the phone began ringing.

With each ring, Brian's heart pounded harder. "C'mon, Angela, pick up."

Finally on the fifth ring, she did.

"It's Brian," he said. "I want you to—" What, he frantically thought, do I tell her that won't scare her to death? "I just had a call from Ivan. He says that Tommy is on the way to your house, and so you might want to leave."

"I'm not letting him in," she said. "But I'm not leaving. Have you looked outside? It's snowing pretty hard."

"Angela, please."

"I'm going to be fine," she said, her voice firm.

"Promise me that you'll call the police if he shows up."

"I can handle—"

"Promise," he demanded.

"Okay," she said after a moment. "I promise."

"Okay."

"Okay," she repeated. "Are we good now?"

They weren't, but he said, "Yes."

The phone disconnected, and the minute it was dead, Brian began to pace. Should he call the police on the basis of Ivan's accusation? Or did he wait? He couldn't sit here and just do nothing. On that thought he called Sam. The phone rang without being answered, while Brian racked his brain trying to remember what Sam had said he'd be doing for the evening, if anything. A movie, he remembered. And so it could be hours before he got back.

Each moment that went by feeling like hours, Brian called for a cab, then groaned in frustration when the dispatcher told him that it might be a half hour before someone could be there. Remembering the line of cabs that were frequently lined up in front of the Marriott a scant five miles from the house, Brian offered the dispatcher a hundred-dollar tip for the driver who could be here in fifteen minutes.

That did the trick. Just a few minutes later, a cab driver knocked on the front door. White cane in hand, Brian left the house and gave the driver Angela's address.

At the other end of town, Tommy was pounding on Angela's door.

And from across the street, Andrew Brogg watched, thinking this was all coming together better than he could have ever imagined.

SEVENTEEN

"**Y**ou gotta talk to me," Tommy yelled through Angela's front door, his words punctuated with his pounding on the door, then repeatedly ringing the bell. "I know you're in there. Open up."

In the kitchen, she picked up the phone and dialed 911.

"What's your emergency?" came the calm voice of the dispatcher over the phone.

"A man is at my front door, demanding I let him in," Angela said, then answered that yes she knew him, yes he was an old boyfriend, no she didn't want him there, yes he was dangerous, no he wasn't threatening her, but yes, she felt threatened. They promised to send someone right away.

Let them get here soon, she prayed as she hung up the phone.

Angela had never heard Tommy like this, upset to the point of being incoherent. Long gone was the guy who had once charmed her so many years ago.

The pounding at the front door abruptly stopped, and she headed into the living room hoping that he'd left.

She didn't see him, but a vehicle she didn't recognize was still parked in front of her house, shrouded by the falling snow.

A second later, she froze as she heard glass breaking and heard the click of the lock, then the back door opening and closing. Brian had been right, she thought through a haze of alarm and macabre surprise. She should have left.

Tommy appeared in the doorway between the living room and kitchen a second later, his corduroy sports coat askew, his hair standing on end and his eyes wild. They stood a long second staring at each other.

"Hey, baby," he said, a lopsided smile not quite erasing his fierce, concentrated expression. He wagged a finger at her. "That wasn't very nice of you to lock me out of the house."

"It's my house," she said, backing away as he sauntered toward her. "You're in here now, so what do you want?" Breathless. She didn't want to sound all out of control like this. She faced him, trying to steady herself.

He raked a shaky hand through the hair falling over his eyebrow. "A beer." The scowl returned. "But you're Miss Goody Two-shoes now, aren't you? I bet you don't have any beer."

"No," she agreed, her voice firmer now. "I don't."

His movements jittery, he came to a stop in the center of the room. Beads of sweat stood out on his forehead. His pupils were constricted, and she realized he was high. She made a wide detour around him, going back to the kitchen. At least he wasn't yelling now. That was something to be thankful for. But since he was under the influence, he also wasn't stable, not by a long shot.

She looked toward the back door and slowly moved it into the kitchen. As soon as he turned his back, she'd make a run for it.

Part of her kept listening for the sound of approaching police. On one hand, the sound of a siren would mean help was near. And on the other, she knew he'd go off the instant he heard them.

Panic blossomed in her chest, and she told herself, "Breathe. Just breathe."

She turned around to find Tommy sitting on one of the kitchen chairs, a hand pressed against his chest, his face contorted. When he caught her watching him, his lips stretched into a mean smile.

"Remember that sweet condo we had in Aspen with the granite counters in the kitchen and the big hot tub on the deck? All within walking distance of the finest shopping in Colorado." He pointed a finger at her, then at himself. "What do you say, doll face? You and me. Enjoying the good times just like we used to?"

"That was a long time ago."

He looked around the kitchen. "Don't expect me to believe you enjoy living like this. I mean, look at this place. It's ugly."

"I like it."

He stood, his eyes wild once more, and she backed away from him.

"You deserve more." The gentle statement was at odds with his fierce expression and his fist once more pressed against the center of his chest.

Despite her resolve and her fear, tears welled in her eyes. "No, actually, I don't."

He looked at her, beginning at her slipper-covered feet to the sweat suit she'd donned to ward off the chill, and finally met her eyes. Nothing was left of the smile, his eyes as hard as she ever remembered them being. "Maybe you don't, but *I* do. And I'm going to have it again. All of it. The nice places to live, the great cars." He took a step closer and sneered. "And the babes, which you clearly aren't anymore."

"Fine." She waved a hand. "Go get it all."

Tommy shook his head. "Not until I get what you owe me. If you held out on Simon Graden, you held out on me."

"I told you—there is no money, Tommy. There never was." She laughed, the sound hysterical in her own ears. "In fact, when the rumor first surfaced I thought you were behind it. If that's what you came here for, you're flat out of luck."

"There's got to be money." His voice rose to a ragged shout. "There has to be money or I'm a dead man. Don't you understand?"

"No."

"I borrowed money from some very bad people. And they want it back. And you're going to help me get it."

"I don't have any."

He stepped forward suddenly and grabbed the cordless telephone from its cradle and thrust it into her hands. "There's always money. You just have to ask." He grabbed her hands and pulled her toward him. "And you're going to ask. Call him."

"Who?"

"Don't be cute, doll face. Your new rich boyfriend."

She pulled away. "You think Brian is a boyfriend? Are you kidding?"

"Yeah. Call him. Now."

She shook her head.

"No is not an option. Dial the number."

"I can't."

"Big difference between can't and won't," he said, dragging her toward the counter where a small bulletin board was tacked to overflowing with papers and notes to herself. "He gave you a card—even I remember that. So it's got to be here somewhere."

"I won't do it."

To her surprise, he let her go. "Want to bet?" He reached into his pocket and pulled out a snub-nosed gun and pointed it at her. "Lady's choice."

Trembling, she stared at Tommy a moment, hating him, God help her, and more frightened than she'd ever been. She dialed Brian's home phone, the number he had dialed her from nearly an hour ago. Too late to remember his begging her to leave. Oh, how she wished she had.

"Hello," came Nonnie's soft voice over the phone.

"Mrs. Ramsey, hi, this is Angela."

"Oh, my goodness, but it's nice to hear your voice. I was just telling Philip how glad we were to have you here last night, especially since Brian told us that we might not see much of you now that Jasper's training is nearly finished. How are you?"

"I'm looking for Brian," she said.

"Well, he's not here," Nonnie said. "I don't know where he is. When he gets home, though, I'll tell him you called."

"Yes, please do that," Angela said, too aware of Tommy waving the gun in her face and asking, "Well, where is he?"

"Not at home," Angela said after disconnecting the call.

"Then call his cell phone. You should have done that first. You're stalling, and you know it."

Halfway through dialing the number, there was a knock at the door.

Tommy's head swiveled toward it. "You expecting anybody?"

"No," she said.

He waved the gun. "Whoever it is, get rid of them."

She hoped it was the police, so she was stunned when she cracked it opened and found Brian on the stoop and a taxi in the driveway.

"You've got to leave," she said, pushing the door mostly closed so Tommy wouldn't see him.

"Is he in there?" Brian demanded.

"Yes," she whispered. "And I did as you asked. Just go. Leave."

"Talk so I can hear you," Tommy demanded from behind her.

"It's just a neighbor," she called back, mentally crossing her fingers against the lie. She pushed against Brian's chest, adding in a louder voice, "I can't visit right now. Maybe tomorrow."

He didn't budge.

She stepped back, intending to close the door in his face, but he pushed hard, and the door bounced open. His white cane in hand, he unerringly stepped into the house.

"Well, well, well," Tommy said, the sneer back in his voice. "You've been lying again. Look at who's shown up just in the nick of time." He waved the gun at Angela. "Get over here, doll face."

To her horror, Brian stepped in front of her. "She's not going anywhere. In fact, she'll be leaving now. With me."

Angela attempted to step around Brian, but was blocked by the half-open door on one side and his steady, reassuring arm on the other. "He's got a gun, Brian."

"I know."

"You're not fooling anyone with that white cane," Tommy said, waving the gun in question. "You can see as well as I do."

"If you say so," Brian agreed, his voice a calm counterpoint to Tommy's increasingly shrill tone.

Once more, Tommy pressed a hand against his chest as his face contorted and more beads of sweat appeared on his forehead. "You write me a check for a half million dollars, and then I'm out of here." He shook his head. "No, that's not gonna work because you could call the bank and stop payment before I cash it."

Brian took a step backward, pushing Angela toward the half-open door. She knew he wanted her to leave, but she couldn't abandon him to face Tommy.

"I'll tell you what," Brian said. "Give me the gun and we'll all go to the bank together in the morning."

"You must think I'm stupid or something," Tommy said, his agitation returning. He swerved, aimed the gun toward the living room window and fired a shot. It reverberated through the room, the window shattering.

Behind Brian, Angela cried out.

He surged forward, swinging his cane like a baseball bat. It hit Tommy squarely with a resounding thud. Tommy swore. Brian reached for him, guided by the sound of his voice and the sheer determination to disarm the man. Finding Tommy's hands, Brian tried to wrestle the gun from his hand. They both fell, and Brian lost his hold on the gun. Brian grabbed once more for Tommy's wrist, and the gun discharged again. When Angela screamed, Brian was sure the bullet had hit her.

He slammed Tommy's hand to the floor again, then again.

Without warning, Tommy suddenly went limp and the gun clattered to the floor. Brian lay on top of the man a moment, unable to judge what had happened. He wasn't ready to relax his grip on Tommy until he knew the man was no longer a threat.

The stench of blood and gunpowder sank into the room.

"Angela," Brian called.

"I'm here."

"Are you all right?"

"Yes, are you?" she answered while he asked, "You're sure?"

"Yes," she repeated, her voice closer.

"That shot didn't hit you?"

"No."

"Then where is all this blood coming from?"

He became aware of sirens in the background growing louder until the sound of them reverberated in his ears.

"Oh, no," Angela said, suddenly next to him. "It's Tommy. And I can't find a pulse."

Silence and a blank emptiness filled Brian's head. He couldn't have killed a man. He couldn't have.

Then, an authoritative voice said, "Step away, and put your hands behind your head."

The hours after that formed into a blur. Brian was separated from Angela, as he was handcuffed and put into the backseat of a police car. After sitting in the dark for what seemed like hours, he was driven to the police station. On the way, he kept asking about Angela, and the officers told him that she was being taken to the county jail. At the station, he was guided into the booking area where he emptied his pockets and gave them his belt, through the booking process where he learned there were no charges against him. That would have been a relief if he had been able to find out any information about Angela.

Several hours later, his attorney, Gil York, picked him up.

"What can you tell me about Angela?" Brian wanted to know as they got into Gil's car.

"You should be asking what happened to Tommy," Gil told him.

"Okay, I'll ask, but I don't care."

"He's dead," Gil said flatly. "And your friend Angela is being held on suspicion of murder."

"She didn't touch the gun," Brian insisted.

"That might be relevant if he'd died of a gunshot wound. We won't know for sure until after the autopsy, but they think he had a heart attack caused by a cocaine overdose."

"What does that have to do with Angela?"

"There's a lot of evidence to suggest they were peddling drugs together, and that Manderoll was his own best customer. Likely, she's an addict, too."

"No," Brian said. "She's not."

"And, given her history, my strong advice is to distance yourself from her. She'll bury you and your foundation."

Though it had been years since the last time she'd been booked, Angela remembered the process when she was delivered to the county jail.

She was allowed to make her phone call. Since it was the middle of the night and since she didn't remember any phone number except Maisey's, she finally settled on leaving Maisey a message on the Guardian Paws answering machine, requesting that she call Micah McLeod and let him know what had happened.

After Angela was placed in the holding cell, she sank down on the metal frame of the bed, staring at the bloodstains on her sweatpants and sweatshirt. She still couldn't believe that Tommy was dead.

She leaned her head against the wall and closed her eyes, remembering that she had reaped what she had sown. Still, she hadn't expected this, to end up back in jail.

"You're still here," an officer said to her sometime later. "I would have thought someone would have come to bail you out by now."

Angela looked at the clock behind the officer and saw that the time was after six. If she were lucky, she'd have only a few more hours before Maisey got her message and put into motion the wheels that would get her out of here.

"We're going to have to transfer you to the jail, you know."

"I know," she replied.

"You made the front page," the officer said, holding up a newspaper.

The bold headline above Andrew Brogg's byline read *The Felon and the Football Player.*

EIGHTEEN

"'The facts about Angela London that we know for sure are these,'" Gramps read from the morning newspaper, sitting across the table from Brian, who was sick with worry for Angela. "'She served time for charges that she pled guilty to related to money laundering and drug trafficking. Her admitted associate for those illegal activities is Thomas J. Manderoll, who was on probation for related charges. Mr. Manderoll suffered a fatal heart attack last night, and the preliminary report from the coroner indicates that it was a result of a cocaine overdose. When Ms. London was released from prison, she'd found a new calling, the training of service dogs. Her current employer is a nonprofit organization, Guardian Paws, which is dependent upon grants and donations.'

"'What we know for sure about Brian Ramsey, retired quarterback for the Patriots, is that he abused anabolic steroids by his own admission. Now that he is retired, Mr. Ramsey's focus is on the work done by his foundation, the Beanstalk Gang, which provides after-school programs for kids throughout the Denver area.

We also know that Val Fitzwater, who is currently serving time for drug trafficking, has sworn under oath that Mr. Ramsey was not only a customer, but a dealer, a charge that he denies. Mr. Ramsey says he has lost his sight, and he recently provided medical affidavits to that effect at a recent news conference. He allegedly met Ms. London when he began his search for a guide dog. And we know that Mr. Manderoll filed a complaint against Mr. Ramsey for assault a couple of weeks ago.'

"'We also know for sure that a minor who has been active with programs at the Beanstalk Gang was recently arrested for allegedly selling drugs to a Denver undercover officer.'" Gramps paused and cleared his throat. "Are you sure you want me to read this whole thing?"

"Every word," Brian assured him. This was nearly as bad as his inability to secure Angela's release, since bail hadn't been set yet.

Nonnie patted his shoulder. "I filled your coffee back up."

"Thanks," Brian told her, then said to his grandfather. "Please read."

Gramps continued to read. The article skewed facts into innuendo that was so farfetched Brian didn't understand how it could have been approved. Brogg made allegations about criminal activity that included wild suppositions linking the Beanstalk Gang and Guardian Paws. Not only was the article fiction, it was slander.

Gramps read, "'The final straw came when Manderoll went to Ms. London's home to pick up money that had been promised to him, money that he owed his Colombian suppliers. What we know for sure is that he had an altercation with Mr. Ramsey at Ms. London's home and that during that altercation, Mr. Manderoll died. What we know for sure is that Mr. Ramsey has been released without any charges being filed against him, once again proving that professional athletes are treated with kid gloves when others in the same situation would be charged with a crime. And we know that as of this writing, Ms. London remains in the county jail with charges pending.'"

"I've heard enough," Brian said, pushing away from the table and stalking out of the kitchen. He headed down the stairs to the weight room, but when he arrived there he simply stood in front of the window where he knew a view of Mount Evans loomed in the distance.

"You okay, Brian?" Sam asked.

Brian could hear the rhythmic sound of the Bowflex machine as Sam went through his routine.

"I'd like to tell you that I'm good," Brian said, "but the truth is that I'm not. The truth…everything has come unraveled, and at the moment I don't have a clue how to put it back together."

The repetitious sound stopped. Brian listened to footfalls come across the room and knew that Sam had come to a stop in front of the window next to him.

"Is this a question of what to do? Or a question of faith?" he asked.

"A little of both."

"You know how it is when the coaches are working on a new play. You plot it out, mentally rehearse it, and then do it."

"Yep," Brian agreed. "You're getting to prayer again."

"I am," Sam said.

"If I just knew where to begin..."

Sam slapped him on the back. "I'm going to go take a shower, and then I'll be ready to take you wherever you decide to go."

"You're sure we're going somewhere?"

"Oh, yeah. We've got a dog to pick up."

Brian had forgotten about the cocker spaniel. He remained standing in front of the window after Sam left. Silently, he began to pray, asking for guidance— to help clear Angela's name, to help her be free of her part once and for all. His eyes closed, he stood there in the silence, listening to the occasional call of a blue jay beyond the window. A feeling of peace came over him that he hadn't expected, a presence so profound he felt tears gather in his eyes.

So this is it, he thought, remembering Angela's calm serenity, and for the first time feeling this for himself. "Thank you, Lord, for this moment," he whispered.

He stood there a while longer, using the techniques he'd learned years ago to center his mind and let it empty of everything, knowing that he'd have clarity when he was finished.

A half hour later, he did, along with an idea of what to do. He pulled out his cell phone, calling first his manager, then his attorney, then Micah McLeod. They had work to do, and he had a Christmas present for Angela that was more important than the cocker spaniel.

* * *

When Angela walked out of the county jail shortly after noon, Maisey, Rachel, Reverend Chester and Micah were waiting for her. She had hoped Maisey would be there, but to find all the people she most cared for waiting—that was something she'd never forget. Grateful beyond words, she was moved to tears. The only person who wasn't there was Brian, but she didn't expect to see him. Not today—perhaps not ever again.

As if sensing she needed someone to lean on, Reverend Chester put his arms around her. "You're going to be just fine."

"You can't go home," Micah told her when Reverend Chester let her go. "Your house is a crime scene."

"So you're coming home with us," Rachel said.

"Why are you doing this?" Angela asked. "Surely you've read the paper, and so you know—"

"That it's a bunch of hogwash," Maisey said, looping an arm through Angela's. "You can't know how sorry I am that I ever thought that Andrew Brogg person was a nice young man."

"And, thanks to his article, he's got some questions to answer," Micah said, guiding them toward the car. "He's been asked to come into the office this afternoon."

"You're not questioning him?"

Micah shook his head. "No. Not since I'm personally involved."

"You don't have to look so bewildered," Rachel said. "Surely you know by now that you're family."

Angela looked back at the woman who had been her

best friend for most of her life, a person with huge reasons to hate her.

Rachel smiled. "The kids will be thrilled to have you stay with us."

"And you?"

"Especially me. It's been too long." She hooked her arm through Angela's. "Though I'm not sure I want to stay up all night and giggle about boys like we used to do."

They began walking toward the car, Angela surrounded by friends. By the only family she'd ever really had. You're too hard on yourself, Brian had told her. It's time you forgive yourself, Reverend Chester had said. Did she dare? She closed her eyes a moment, testing what that might feel like, and it was as though she had been hiding within the shadows and just now dared to step into the sunshine.

Despite the problems facing Guardian Paws as a result of Andrew's article, Angela knew she wanted the sunshine.

"We've got some shopping to do," Rachel said. "You can't spend Christmas week in your sweatpants."

"I have my credit card all warmed up," Maisey said.

Too full of joy and gratitude to express it, Angela looked from Rachel to Maisey. "We're ruined...again, I might add, so you might want to hold on to your cash."

"Not this time," Micah said. "Have a little faith. You haven't done anything wrong, and if I have anything to say about it, Andrew Brogg will be revealed for the liar he is."

"I rescheduled Jasper's final testing for Monday," Maisey said.

Angela stared at her. "I'd forgotten. And I can't believe that."

At Angela's bewildered tone, Maisey laughed. "We'd noticed that you had a couple of things on your mind. And I called Brian, too. I didn't talk to him, but his grandmother says he's fine."

One more thing to be thankful for, Angela thought. She was surrounded by friends, and Brian was okay. They all had a mess to deal with, but she had to believe that things would somehow work out for the best.

It was late Saturday afternoon before Angela was able to get back into her house. Someone had put plywood over the broken living room window and over the broken glass in the back door. The inside was pretty much a mess, though, between the litter left behind by the EMTs in their efforts to revive Tommy and the things that had been knocked over during Brian and Tommy's struggle. Maisey and Rachel had both come with her, and Angela admitted she was happy she didn't have to be alone in the house. Given the way Tommy had died, she wasn't sure she would ever be able to live here again.

Gathering up the few things she wanted, including the Christmas presents she had purchased, they headed back to Rachel's house.

Angela awoke very early on Sunday morning and made her way downstairs where she found the morning coffee already brewing. When she saw the newspaper on the front step, she stood in indecision a moment, remembering the searing pain she'd felt over the story published in Friday's paper. Deciding it was unlikely anything that bad would be in today's, she brought it inside and unfolded it on the kitchen table.

Below the fold was a headline that made her heart pound. Andrew Brogg Fired.

The article that followed had a careful wording that suggested an attorney had crafted it to minimize the possibility of any lawsuit. The gist of it was that while some of the facts that had been quoted in the article were true, most of the story was a fabrication. Talks with Andrew Brogg had revealed he had entered into negotiations with a major publisher for a tell-all book about Mr. Ramsey. The article concluded with, "Ms. London has paid her debt to society, and there is zero evidence to suggest that she has been anything other than a model citizen since her release from prison. According to her business partner, Maisey Erdmann, 'The positive impact Angela has had on Guardian Paws cannot be overstated.' Further, the managing editor of this newspaper stands behind the article published last November about the Beanstalk Gang and the good work being done by Mr. Ramsey through this organization."

Stunned and once more thankful beyond words, Angela stared at the print until it blurred. This was so much more than she had dared hope for. She had anticipated it would be years before her name and Brian's were cleared.

"Auntie Angela," Sarah exclaimed, skipping across the kitchen. Soon to be ten, she reminded Angela so much of Rachel when they had been that age. "You're up." Her voice lowered to a conspiratorial whisper. "Usually, I'm the first one up, and it's my quiet time without my little brother."

Angela chuckled. "I see."

Sarah gave her a hug. "I'm glad you're going to be here all week. It's going to be just like having a real aunt."

When yet another lump rose in Angela's throat and her eyes once more blurred, she blamed it on the season. And that might have almost worked as a rationalization if she hadn't become teary during the church service where she was once more surrounded by people she loved.

The following morning, Angela headed for Guardian Paws early, anticipating the day and the successful conclusion to Jasper's training. She had no doubt. By this afternoon, he would be a certified guide dog. Maisey was already there, humming Christmas carols under her breath when Angela came into the kitchen.

"Ready or not," Maisey said with a grin. "Only one more week until Christmas. I feel so fortunate I was able to talk the inspector into rescheduling Jasper's test for this morning. I thought for sure we'd have to wait until after the first of the year."

"I'm glad we don't," Angela responded. "I'm going to miss Jasper something fierce, though."

"I can imagine."

She looked toward the backyard where the dogs were playing, her memory drawn to the first morning that Brian had come to see them. Since then Polly, Gatsby, and Bailey had gone to their new jobs. Jasper would be leaving this afternoon, which left only Checkers and the boxer she had adopted the last day she had spent with Brian. The boxer had such a regal presence that she had named him Baron. He was answering to his name, and she had high hopes for his training, though it was too soon to tell whether he'd make the cut.

"I have a confession," Maisey said. When Angela looked at her, she added, "Dina Jackson is coming out here this morning."

Angela frowned. "The name rings a bell—"

"She's the anchor of that morning show, *Great Day Denver.*"

"No, Maisey. Not again." Angela backed away. "We've done enough of this."

Maisey reached for her arm. "I promise. This time it's going to be okay. She called me on Saturday, and we had a long talk. When I expressed my doubts, she invited me to come down to the station and see what she was working on, and I did. The piece is going to air this Friday, and it's all about people who personify the giving spirit of Christmas." Maisey gave her a soft smile. "Sweetie, don't you get it? That's you."

Before Angela had time even to absorb what Maisey had just said, Dina and her cameraman arrived. A little makeup and a fluff to her hair, and somehow she was outside, demonstrating the two ends of the training spectrum for Dina: Jasper, who was an hour away from taking his final test to get his certification, and Baron, who was at the very beginning of his training.

When they were finished, and the dogs were sitting obediently at Angela's feet, Dina said, "Watching you work with these dogs is one of the most wonderful things ever. I'm so glad Brian called me and told me this would be the perfect finale for my show before the Christmas break."

Angela shook her head in confusion. "You mean Brian Ramsey?"

Dina laughed. "The very same. He said I'd meet a remarkable woman and the dog that was going to help him keep his independence."

"When was this?" Angela asked.

"Last Friday. And after he told me about what had really happened rather than the Andrew Brogg version, I told him I'd love to talk to you." She paused. "There won't be any mention of that story, I give you my word."

"This is wonderful, and I'm thankful, but why—"

"Am I doing this?" Dina smiled. "I've known Brian since we were in high school together, and he's one of the good guys, you know? When I needed help for my big break, he was there. When he told me about you, I wanted to do the story."

They continued to chat while the cameraman got some additional shots of the facility. Through it, Angela's focus remained on the surprising fact that Brian had arranged this.

And she had been convinced that he'd never again want anything to do with her, which she told Maisey after Dina left.

"That wouldn't explain why the man has pestered the life out of me the last few days wanting to make sure you're all right." Maisey grinned. "He said he'd be here after lunch to pick up Jasper."

NINETEEN

"You are the most handsome boy ever," Angela told Jasper while she brushed his curly hair. "No purple hair left anywhere, and I doubt you'll ever wear a Continental cut again."

He watched her with wide, intelligent eyes that seemed to understand what she was saying. They were in the workroom in the small barn of Guardian Paws. Baron was sprawled on the floor, taking a nap.

"Not only are you handsome," Angela continued, "but smart, too. And now you get to do the work you were meant to do."

They had finished the test, and Jasper had passed with flying colors just as she had known he would, navigating his way through downtown Denver like the pro that he was.

If she only had one ounce of that same confidence for herself. Brian was due to arrive soon, and she was nervous. Telling herself that it was only a little adrenaline was a bit like saying she was only a little in love with him.

The man had gone to a lot of trouble, so she had

to believe that meant he felt what she did. But what if she had read the signals all wrong, and what if he didn't? After all, she'd told him often enough that things wouldn't—couldn't—work out for them.

Despite his coming to her rescue last Thursday night.

"What if I'm wrong, Jasper?" she whispered, dropping her face against his soft hair.

She heard the outside door open, and she lifted her head, her heart suddenly pounding.

"I'm back here," she called, hoping she sounded casual, tempted to run to the door and launch herself into Brian's arms if he was the one who had just come into the barn.

Baron lifted his head, then padded to the open doorway of the workroom, his head cocked to the side as he looked at whomever it was who had come in. But just as he had been trained, he didn't bark and didn't move beyond the mental boundary she had set for him.

"Good boy," she praised, then came to the door, still so nervous she couldn't stand it.

No Brian.

Instead, a small buff and honey-colored cocker spaniel wearing an enormous red bow sat just inside the doorway. When he saw her, he yelped a happy bark and sped toward her as fast as his feet would carry him, launching himself into her arms. He wriggled in her arms, licking her face as though they were long-lost friends that hadn't seen each other in forever.

"Merry Christmas, Angela," Brian said from the doorway, his voice deeper than usual.

She looked from him to the dog, then back at him. "The dog—"

"His name is Ziggy." The white cane tapping confidently in front of him, Brian moved toward her. "The last time you saw him he didn't look...or smell...this good."

"This is the one from the shelter that broke my heart!"

"It is."

"How— When?"

"The day after we saw him. He's been to the vet and all checked out. The shelter thought he was heartworm positive, but the vet says he isn't. He's about five years old, and he's in good health."

"A companion for Jasper," she murmured. "When he's not working, he'll like that."

Brian took a breath. "Actually, this guy has a different job in store." He took a step closer to her. "His job is to make sure you don't ever again come home to an empty house."

"He's mine?" Her voice choked, the memory of that Christmas years earlier when she had asked for a dog at the surface.

"Yours," Brian said.

"You got me a dog?"

Her voice was filled with such wonder that Brian smiled, seeing her in his mind's eye, her face lit in the soft smile he had loved so much.

"How did you know?" she asked.

"You told me," he said simply. "We may have a problem, though, since Maisey told me that you're not staying at your house right now, which I should have figured, but didn't."

"I don't think Rachel will mind," she said. "Plus, this might provide me with motivation to get back home more quickly."

"This dog comes with stuff," Brian said,

"What kind of stuff?" she wanted to know.

"I'll show you in a minute. Now, don't keep me in suspense any longer. How did Jasper do?"

"He did great, of course. Call him, and he'll tell you himself."

Brian knelt on one knee and called his dog. A second later, he felt Jasper's head butt against his hand, the familiar curly hair against his palm. "Is that right? You're a certified guide dog?"

As if answering yes, he felt the dog's head move beneath his hand.

"And you get your dog just in time for Christmas," she said.

There was some emotion in her voice that he couldn't read. A wistfulness maybe.

He was a man who had always gone after what he wanted with intensity and determination. All of that seemed beyond him right at the moment since telling her what was in his heart meant laying it bare. He knew she felt a connection, but she had put him off so many times, he wasn't sure in this moment whether it was something in himself or in her past that had to be overcome. And the idea that she might shoot him down again...he didn't even want to go there.

"Brian, I...uh..." There it was. That wistful uncertainty again, when she'd had none during all the weeks of training Jasper.

"What's on your mind, coach?"

She laughed, a strangled sound. "I don't feel much like a coach at the moment."

"What do you feel like?"

"An idiot who can't figure out what to say next."

She sounded close, so he extended his hand. A moment later, hers slipped within his, fragile compared to his bigger one. He knew the fragility was an illusion since he'd seen her skillfully control the dogs she was training.

Standing, he said, "Is there someplace to sit?"

She tugged on his hand and led him to the center aisle that ran down the middle of the barn. "There's a bench right here," she said, "a foot or so in front of your shins."

He sat down without letting go of her hand, and when he figured out that the bench was set against one of the dog cages, leaned his back against it. "I always liked this place," he said, remembering the expectant faces of the dogs when he'd come in here with Angela.

"Jasper is waiting for you to call him." She sank down next to him. He liked this. Shoulder-to-shoulder.

"Come here, boy," he said and was rewarded a moment later when he felt the dog settle at his feet. She laughed, and he asked, "What's going on?"

"Ziggy just scared himself. He stepped on the pedal of the wastebasket and when it gave way he jumped. That of course made the lid snap down, which scared him again."

"Ah. A sight gag."

"Yeah." She sighed. "Sorry."

"Don't be." He squeezed her hand.

"Brian…"

"Hmm."

"The other night…thank you for coming."

"You're welcome."

"No one ever rescued me before."

"Not ever?"

"No. I guess, what I'm trying to say is that I liked it—having someone I can depend on. Only, I've been on my own such a long time that I'm not very good at it. And—"

"Angela, what are you trying to say?"

"I…I…"

"Just say the words. What's the worst that could happen?"

"My heart might break."

He clasped her hand more tightly.

"I love you," she whispered.

He took a deep breath, savoring the moment. It was as sweet as he had imagined.

Standing, he pulled Angela to her feet and into his arms, then kissed her. Once. Twice. And again, each touch a promise that she was lovable just as she was. "I love you," he said between the kisses he sprinkled over her cheeks. "I think I have from that very first day."

Ziggy jumped on her legs, demanding attention from first her and then Brian.

"Maybe I should just keep him with me so he doesn't

get all confused about where home is," he said, "since he'll be living at my house after we're married."

Angela swatted him on the shoulder. "Tell me that wasn't a proposal."

He reached for her hand and brought her fingers to his lips. "Yeah, it was." A ring appeared from between his fingers. "Some things a guy doesn't want to leave to chance. I bought this a couple of days after we went shopping for dishes."

She could hardly see for the tears swimming in her eyes, but it was beautiful, the oval diamond surrounded by two smaller stones.

"I can take it back if you don't like it."

"No." She held out her hand so he'd feel her fingers butting against the ring. "You can't."

He slid the ring on her finger, and then she wrapped her arms tight around him, gratitude once more filling her heart. She had risen from the ashes of her past, and it was good in every way.

* * * * *

Dear Reader,

Have you ever wanted a "do over"? I sure have. This was one of the underlying ideas of this book. Over the course of the story, Angela and Brian are dealing with the results of poor choices made in their pasts. If asked, I'd bet, they'd like a "do over," too.

That led me to think about Debbie Ford's book *The Right Questions,* in which she encourages us to consider the consequences of our decisions by asking, *Does this choice empower me or disempower me?* I find the most disempowering choices to be the ones we fall into when we're not paying attention—whether it's ordering fries and a burger instead of that healthier salad or driving too fast.

My hope for you is that you find and make those choices that empower you. May God's blessing be always with you and yours.

Sharon Mignerey

Discussion Questions

1. Angela and Brian each have a tarnished past. What are the differences between them in how they deal with their respective histories?

2. Both Angela and Brian are propelled toward acts of community service as a way to find redemption. What biblical examples reinforce this idea?

3. When Angela and Brian discuss the benefits of prayer, she indicates she believes all prayers are answered, and encourages him to test whether his are. Do you think this is a right idea? Why or why not? What biblical references support your view?

4. Would Tommy have come to the same end if Andrew hadn't been manipulating him? Why do you think so?

5. One of the themes in this book is redemption. How does this play out in the story? How does this fit with your ideas about redemption?

6. Another theme in the book is being responsible for your own actions. What elements in the story demonstrate this for Angela, Brian, Tommy and Andrew?

7. Brian talks to himself several times in his closet, using the space as a confessional, of sorts. What

do these moments signify to you and how does this fit with what Jesus says in *Matthew* 6:6?

8. What parallels do you see between walking in faith and walking with a guide dog? What does the Bible say about walking in faith?

9. Angela's faith doesn't initially include forgiving herself. How does that play out in the story and how does that cause her to limit herself?

10. Does Brian's faith happen at once or creep up little by little? What examples demonstrate his growing faith?

REQUEST YOUR FREE BOOKS!

2 FREE INSPIRATIONAL NOVELS
PLUS 2
FREE
MYSTERY GIFTS

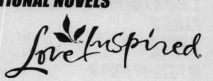

REQUEST YOUR FREE BOOKS!

2 FREE INSPIRATIONAL NOVELS
PLUS 2
FREE
MYSTERY GIFTS

Love Inspired
HISTORICAL
INSPIRATIONAL HISTORICAL ROMANCE

YES! Please send me 2 FREE Love Inspired® Historical novels and my 2 FREE mystery gifts (gifts are worth about $10). After receiving them, if I don't wish to receive any more books, I can return the shipping statement marked "cancel." If I don't cancel, I will receive 4 brand-new novels every month and be billed just $4.49 per book in the U.S. or $4.99 per book in Canada. That's a savings of at least 22% off the cover price. It's quite a bargain! Shipping and handling is just 50¢ per book in the U.S. and 75¢ per book in Canada.* I understand that accepting the 2 free books and gifts places me under no obligation to buy anything. I can always return a shipment and cancel at any time. Even if I never buy another book, the two free books and gifts are mine to keep forever.

102/302 IDN FV2V

Name _____ (PLEASE PRINT) _____

Address _____ Apt. # _____

City _____ State/Prov. _____ Zip/Postal Code _____

Signature (if under 18, a parent or guardian must sign) _____

Mail to the Harlequin® Reader Service:
IN U.S.A.: P.O. Box 1867, Buffalo, NY 14240-1867
IN CANADA: P.O. Box 609, Fort Erie, Ontario L2A 5X3

Want to try two free books from another series?
Call 1-800-873-8635 or visit www.ReaderService.com.

* Terms and prices subject to change without notice. Prices do not include applicable taxes. Sales tax applicable in N.Y. Canadian residents will be charged applicable taxes. Offer not valid in Quebec. This offer is limited to one order per household. Not valid for current subscribers to Love Inspired Historical books. All orders subject to credit approval. Credit or debit balances in a customer's account(s) may be offset by any other outstanding balance owed by or to the customer. Please allow 4 to 6 weeks for delivery. Offer available while quantities last.

Your Privacy—The Harlequin® Reader Service is committed to protecting your privacy. Our Privacy Policy is available online at www.ReaderService.com or upon request from the Harlequin Reader Service.

We make a portion of our mailing list available to reputable third parties that offer products we believe may interest you. If you prefer that we not exchange your name with third parties, or if you wish to clarify or modify your communication preferences, please visit us at www.ReaderService.com/consumerschoice or write to us at Harlequin Reader Service Preference Service, P.O. Box 9062, Buffalo, NY 14269. Include your complete name and address.

LIHDIR13

REQUEST YOUR FREE BOOKS!

2 FREE RIVETING INSPIRATIONAL NOVELS
PLUS 2 FREE MYSTERY GIFTS

Love Inspired.
SUSPENSE

YES! Please send me 2 FREE Love Inspired® Suspense novels and my 2 FREE mystery gifts (gifts are worth about $10). After receiving them, if I don't wish to receive any more books, I can return the shipping statement marked "cancel." If I don't cancel, I will receive 4 brand-new novels every month and be billed just $4.49 per book in the U.S. or $4.99 per book in Canada. That's a savings of at least 22% off the cover price. It's quite a bargain! Shipping and handling is just 50¢ per book in the U.S. and 75¢ per book in Canada.* I understand that accepting the 2 free books and gifts places me under no obligation to buy anything. I can always return a shipment and cancel at any time. Even if I never buy another book, the two free books and gifts are mine to keep forever.

123/323 IDN FVZV

Name		(PLEASE PRINT)	

Address			Apt. #

City	State/Prov.	Zip/Postal Code

Signature (if under 18, a parent or guardian must sign)

Mail to the **Harlequin® Reader Service:**
IN U.S.A.: P.O. Box 1867, Buffalo, NY 14240-1867
IN CANADA: P.O. Box 609, Fort Erie, Ontario L2A 5X3

**Are you a subscriber to Love Inspired Suspense
and want to receive the larger-print edition?
Call 1-800-873-8635 or visit www.ReaderService.com.**

* Terms and prices subject to change without notice. Prices do not include applicable taxes. Sales tax applicable in N.Y. Canadian residents will be charged applicable taxes. Offer not valid in Quebec. This offer is limited to one order per household. Not valid for current subscribers to Love Inspired Suspense books. All orders subject to credit approval. Credit or debit balances in a customer's account(s) may be offset by any other outstanding balance owed by or to the customer. Please allow 4 to 6 weeks for delivery. Offer available while quantities last.

Your Privacy—The Harlequin® Reader Service is committed to protecting your privacy. Our Privacy Policy is available online at www.ReaderService.com or upon request from the Harlequin Reader Service.
We make a portion of our mailing list available to reputable third parties that offer products we believe may interest you. If you prefer that we not exchange your name with third parties, or if you wish to clarify or modify your communication preferences, please visit us at www.ReaderService.com/consumerschoice or write to us at Harlequin Reader Service Preference Service, P.O. Box 9062, Buffalo, NY 14269. Include your complete name and address.

LISDIR13